CAUGHT LOOKING

Also by Alison Tyler

Best Bondage Erotica
Best Bondage Erotica 2
Exposed
The Happy Birthday Book of Erotica
Heat Wave: Sizzling Sex Stories
Luscious: Stories of Anal Eroticism
The Merry XXXmas Book of Erotica
Red Hot Erotica
Slave to Love
Three-Way: Erotic Stories

CAUGHT LOOKING

EROTIC STORIES OF EXHIBITIONISTS
AND VOYEURS

EDITED BY
RACHEL KRAMER BUSSEL & ALISON TYLER

CLEIS
PRESS

Published in the United States by Cleis Press Inc.,
P.O. Box 14697, San Francisco, California 94114.

Printed in the United States.
Cover design: Scott Idleman
Cover photograph: Patryce Bak
Text design: Frank Wiedemann
Cleis Press logo art: Juana Alicia
First Edition.
10 9 8 7 6 5 4 3 2

An exhibitionist is nothing without a voyeur.
—S. SACHS

The exhibitionist loves to flirt with shame.
—MASON COOLEY

Acknowledgments

Rachel Kramer Bussel would like to thank Bess Abrahams, Allison Bojarski, Miriam Datskovsky, Ellen Friedrichs, Zak Nelson, Lori Perkins, Barbara Pizio, Devan Sagliani, Heidi Schmid, and Nichelle Stephens for all their support and encouragement. An extra special anonymous thanks to the person who inspired her story.

Alison Tyler would like to thank SAM, who always watches.

The authors would like to thank Felice Newman and Frédérique Delacoste for wholeheartedly supporting this project and all its sexy possibilities.

Contents

ix   *Introduction: Exposing the Exhibitionist* •
ALISON TYLER

xiii   *Introduction: Confessions of a Confirmed Voyeur* •
RACHEL KRAMER BUSSEL

1   *Curtain Call* • THOMAS S. ROCHE

11   *Room with a View* • SASKIA WALKER

21   *A Flash of Gold* • RADCLYFFE

31   *All Eyes on Her* • M. CHRISTIAN

35   *Walled Lake Girl* • TARA ALTON

45   *Tight Spots* • DEBRA HYDE

57   *Replacements* • TENILLE BROWN

65   *The Changing Room* • CATHERINE LUNDOFF

79   *My Finest Hour* • STAN KENT

93   *The Stars Fell Down* • KRISTINA WRIGHT

103   *Couples Welcome* • ERICA DUMAS

111   *Busted* • SOPHIE MOUETTE

125   *X-ray Specs* • HEATHER PELTIER

135   *Forceful Personalities* • DOMINIC SANTI

147   *The Poet, Dying* • SIMON SHEPPARD

157   *Command Performance* • TERESA NOELLE ROBERTS

165   *The Key* • SAGE VIVANT

177   *Down on Your Knees* • SHANNA GERMAIN

187   *Late Bloomer* • ALISON TYLER

201   *Sharing the Perfect Cock* • RACHEL KRAMER BUSSEL

217   *About the Authors*

223   *About the Editors*

EXPOSING THE EXHIBITIONIST

Alison Tyler

Watch me.

Put me on display. That's what I like. Doll me up and take me out. I'll be your pony girl, with glossy leather boots riding all the way up to my slender thighs. I'll be your naughty school-girl, in a kinky blue-and-green-plaid skirt and shiny high-heeled Mary Janes. I'll be your siren in shimmering satin, or your vixen dressed down in my favorite pair of beat-up Levi's. Truthfully, I don't care what sort of clothes you put me in. I only want you to dress me up and take me out, so that people can watch.

I've always been this way. Yes, I come across as shy at first, with my dark brown eyes cast down; my shoulder-length hair falling forward, hiding my face. I have a long-standing habit of biting my full lower lip when nervous or excited. But all of that's an act. What I want most are eyes on me. What I *crave* is the excitement I feel when I know others are watching.

And they are. They *always* are. They've been watching from the very start.

There were eyes on me when Alexander backed me up against the wall behind the record store where he worked, sliding one hand along the lean line of my body, pulling my summery dress up to reveal my lavender lace-edged panties. People could see us when Jack and I had sex in the back row of the theater, my long leather jacket open, my short navy skirt hiked to my slim waist. And when Sam and I fucked in that club in Paris, we gave a thrill to every voyeur who strolled by.

"Open your eyes," Sam said. "They're watching you."

And he was right. They were.

My heart pounded as I made eye contact with the other patrons. As they gazed at us for their personal viewing pleasure, staring at the place where our bodies met, then looking up into my eyes and letting me know that they saw.

I want to be seen. All the time. Everywhere. It goes deeper than that.

I *need* you to stare at me, to see me. To watch the way my face changes, my expressions shift. To see the subtle strength that pulses in my eyes. To see the defiance there, the power that makes me who I am—the real person behind the shy exterior.

Watch me.

But when you stop, when you tear yourself away, I'll still be there, my back arched, my lips parted. You'll feel me gazing at you—and you'll look back, and then *I'll* be the one watching you. We can take turns, like the authors in this collection. The voyeurs and the exhibitionists, playing hide and seek with the sultry characters in their sexy tales. From Thomas S. Roche's delicious "Curtain Call" to M. Christian's intoxicating "All Eyes on Her," there are other lads and lasses here like me who need to be seen. And from Saskia Walker's naughty heroines in "Room with a View" to the voyeur in Tenille Brown's "Replacements," there are other lovers who delight in doing the seeing.

I'm sure you'll be won over with both—and I'll know. Because, just like you, I'll be watching.

CONFESSIONS OF A CONFIRMED VOYEUR

Rachel Kramer Bussel

I can't lie—I like to watch. Looking at sexy people exulting in their sensuality, playing it up, flirting, flaunting it, gets me hot. Knowing they want to show off for me makes it all the better. I live in New York, the ultimate city for people watching, but only rarely do I actually get to engage in true voyeurism—watching other people have sex.

Sometimes I attend sex parties, where a giant room might be filled with all sorts of couplings. But the action that gets me hottest isn't the most over-the-top scene in the room, but one where I see two people so lost in each other that their bodies seem to give off waves of heat, a magnetism that's enough to lure anyone into their web. Once, during a threesome with a private sex party's host couple, I remember watching them kiss as the three of us were entangled and being both awed and jealous of the passion their lips shared, until they opened their circle to include me, letting me peek, and join in. I also like it when lovers show off just for me, and I have asked several I know to show me how they touch themselves when I'm not around. Watching as their fingers stroke and pump makes me feel like I'm being let into a secret world, given a special lens to view the utterly private.

Like talking dirty, another sexual act I indulge in every chance I get, watching uses one of my senses to enhance another. Seeing a lover strip for me, watching him run his hands up and down his body; making her display her masturbation techniques, showing off the bite marks or reddened skin from a spanking; checking out her cleavage or his ass from across the room when they don't know I'm looking—all of this gets me hot and makes my body purr. Time seems to stop as I soak in her curves, his tattoos, her strong back, his neck, her parted lips, his hard cock. Whatever position I'm in, I like to watch as our bodies melt against each other, and that visual is like a show-within-a-show for me, its impact spurring on my desire.

The authors who've graced us with their naughty tales here also share the thrill of watching—and being watched. I'm not so much a spy as I am a blatant voyeur; I like the people I'm watching to know I'm looking, to feel my gaze as they bare their innermost selves to me. I like to watch people's faces when they come, when every last shred of inhibition gets tossed out and they are naked, bare, caught in my glance. I like them to feel my eyes burning into them, warming them; to know I'm getting off by absorbing whatever it is they want to reveal. When they're strutting their stuff just for me, giving me visual cues that tell me they know I've got my gaze pinned on them, I'm in heaven, squirreling away those images in my mind to replay later; responding to their every move, whether they're flirting from across the room, masturbating on command, or making love to someone else before my eyes.

Stan Kent knows exactly what I'm talking about, and he shares his voyeuristic secrets in "My Finest Hour." Once you read his story, I bet you'll want to watch his protagonist's lover, who knows just how to make sure you'll stick around to see what she'll do next. He puts us right at the heart of why looking is so alluring: "Notice how the word *shower* contains *show*. Show and shower—the two go together like a wet pussy and a stiff cock. Our glassed enclosure is her stage...my luxurious private and personal peep show that satisfies my fundamental sexual need to watch my lover engaged in what would be private and personal moments if it weren't for the fact that I'm watching." Watching someone in the throes of ecstasy, watching him surrender, fully and completely, to those stirring rumblings inside, is a powerful thrill. I consider it an honor, a gift, whether that means a breast flashed at me on the sly, or a private masturbation ritual that I'm let in on. I replay the memories of watching when I'm alone, a special erotic reel looping forever in my mind.

Other stories here also delight in the voyeuristic nature of sex. Tara Alton's "Walled Lake Girl" likes to check out her naughty neighbor as he fucks countless girls, until the tables get turned and she's the one in his bedroom while someone else (possibly) peeks in.

Despite our title, you don't need to be *caught* looking—you can unabashedly enjoy every second of these personal peep shows that take you into a world where lovers light up their bedroom stages, creating dramas worthy of the big screen, whether it's a slow reveal or an all-out erotic extravaganza. Join us—and look to your heart's content. I know I will.

CURTAIN CALL

Thomas S. Roche

We should get one thing straight from the outset: Drew wasn't in the habit of taking her clothes off in front of strangers. Sure, she might have thought about it once or twice, but she never figured she'd actually do it. *Especially* not strangers who knew where she lived.

She'd been a little uncomfortable when she'd first taken the apartment; it was weird for her, a country girl, to be living in the city with a picture window right across the alley from another apartment. The rental agent had explained that this apartment building had been built before the other one—that once the picture window had looked out over a beautiful view of the lake. But a few years ago, the high-rise had gone up across the alley, and now the view was of some other person's living room. Not that it had inspired the landlord to lower the rent or anything— but Drew didn't care; she was just glad to have an apartment after her long and frustrating search.

Besides, the second she'd seen the picture window facing the apartment across the alley, her mind had turned to the idea of taking her clothes off in front of it, and the deal was closed. Not that she thought she'd actually do it, mind you. Drew wasn't exactly a good girl; in fact she really wasn't a good girl; in fact, she wasn't anything even remotely like a good girl, but she drew the line at taking her clothes off in public. Her provocative clothing was nothing more than a matter of physical geography, albeit one she relished. She didn't go out of her way to display her full hips, her large breasts, her thick, strong legs—they just sort of displayed themselves, and she liked it that way. Drew's tasteful office attire was always a little dressier than was necessary, maybe even slightly tighter than was necessary, showing off the swell of her tits and the curves of her ass. It never crossed the line of propriety, mind you, not quite "slutty," just, how would you say it, "body-comfortable"—that worked. She drew more approving looks than she would have thought possible when she was the quote-unquote "overweight" ugly duckling living in Wisketaw, Minnesota. Funny how that happened.

Guys at the office were always asking her for dates, but after all, Drew had moved here to "find" herself, that obscure thing people were supposed to do when they turned twenty-five or maybe twenty-nine, or in Drew's case twenty-seven, two years late or early, depending on your perspective.

So Drew turned her admirers down for their dinners and movies and impossible-to-get seats at *Miss Saigon*—and stayed home, reveling in the pleasures of her new apartment. And the pleasures of that big picture window.

Drew would stay home weekend nights, often having turned down a date or two from the technicians up on the fifth floor or the lawyers on seven—most of the bastards married—or once, even, the FedEx dude, who she'd been sure was gay. She just couldn't stand the thought of going through another love affair when she finally had an apartment to herself, a place where she could stretch out on the expansive, luxurious floor—more luxurious than a couch would have been, even had she been able to afford one—and ease out of her office clothes, enjoying the sight of herself in the big mirror on the closet door, enjoying the sight of her sexy garter belt, stockings, tight panties, sometimes even no panties, the knowledge of that making her uncomfortably but deliciously wet all day long. She could put a porn movie in the VCR, one of those "women's erotica" movies she'd discovered at the feminist porn shop recently. The porn was disgustingly PC compared to the sleaze her ex-boyfriends used to want to watch with her, but yet it was somehow unbelievably sexy precisely because it was aimed at her, like it represented the fact that everyone in the world knew she was masturbating right now—or something. She would put on one of the movies and stretch out on the floor with a bottle of red wine and her vibrator and maybe even a dildo or two, enjoying the feeling of being horribly, terribly, irrevocably bad—not because she was watching porn or masturbating with sex toys, but because she was drinking red wine on that immaculate white carpet, and her anxiety about losing part of her cleaning deposit was matched only by the decadent thrill she felt in thinking about dumping the whole bottle over her naked body and laughing about it, and because she was going to be alone in this apartment for a long, delicious time.

Drew would keep the curtains closed on that window, thinking about who might be beyond it, thinking about what they were doing. Maybe the people who lived there had their curtains open and were doing nasty things in front of the window, wishing Drew would open her curtains so she could see them. The thought gave her a thrill. Drew was as much a closet voyeur as a closet exhibitionist. Once when she lived in Minnesota she'd heard her downstairs neighbors fucking. She'd fantasized about that for months, still fantasized about it sometimes when she was masturbating. When she'd found out, weeks later, that *two women* lived there, a handsome diesel dyke and a curvy femme, that only fueled Drew's savoring of her illicit carnal knowledge. There's something so delicious about things you're not supposed to know, like what two lesbians sound like in the throes of lovemaking.

Now, she would fantasize about the people on the other side of those curtains. She would think about them watching her as she looked at porn and stroked herself; as she spread her broad thighs; as she tugged her skimpy panties to one side and slipped the silicone dildo smoothly into her body; as she turned the vibrator on HIGH and pressed it to her clit; as she came, screaming, to the images on the TV screen and the knowledge of sexual beings right behind her curtains, wanting to watch her and being denied. More than once Drew left her window open behind those closed curtains, watching the red fabric ripple in the twenty-fifth-floor breeze, knowing that wind might carry her orgasmic screams to the people across the alley, or—and this never failed to get her off—the people *in* the alley many floors below.

But Drew never actually *opened* the curtains—not even when she was just hanging out—to see who lived there. That might have spoiled the fantasy, she figured. Or would it?

Drew discovered her very favorite video one night when she was just a little tipsy from a glass of wine and pleasantly satisfied by take-out Chateaubriand from Francesca's Italian Restaurant—she'd just gotten a midmonth paycheck and wanted to treat herself. There wasn't a bit of irony in her liking it, because

Drew watched a lot of videos, having grown up in a place where "women's erotica" meant *Cosmopolitan* articles on "How to Give Your Man Orgasms!" At this point, she'd seen practically every so-called "sex-positive" video, both lesbian and straight, that the sex shop rented, and she was starting in on the commercial stuff out of sheer desperation. But somehow she'd missed *The Hungry Gaze* in her first whirlwind tour through the video section. It had been made by a tiny lesbian erotica company in Minneapolis. The company's location was an interesting coincidence, to be sure, and one that would drive Drew to even more perverse fantasies of sexual exhibition. But given how many videos Drew had watched since moving to the city, there really wasn't that much irony in her response.

That is to say, in the fact that *The Hungry Gaze* was a thirty-minute short about a woman who showed off for her female neighbor in front of the picture window of her high-rise apartment building.

Drew came three times, the remains of the Chateaubriand forgotten, the red wine serving only to hydrate her in gulps taken between her frenzied bursts of self-fucking and desperate rewinding of the tape, muttering, "Come on, come on," while she stroked her wet pussy and listened to the annoying whine of the VCR. Then she started all over again.

It didn't bother her one bit that the woman on the tape was showing off for another woman, despite the fact that Drew thought of herself as exclusively straight. Hell, the woman across the alley in the video was more handsome than any of Drew's boyfriends had been, and the woman showing off looked more like Drew than the blow-dried prom queens she usually saw in commercial porn and even a lot of the more artistic stuff. Her yummy broad ass and rounded hips were cinched lusciously into a corset, her luscious tits spilling out with their bright rings dancing for the camera as the woman ground her hips and spread her legs, exposing her shaved pussy as she slipped her fingers inside. The woman across the alley, a skinny dyke with a DA, lay naked except for a stained jockstrap, fondling her small tits and pulling the cotton garment away so she could rub her pussy as she watched. The tension between the two women, even across the illusory gap between buildings, was palpable and drove Drew into a new fury.

"Fuck," muttered Drew hungrily as she pumped her pussy yet again. "Sign me up."

But what really turned her on was the fact that the woman was showing off—and doing it in front of a window. It made Drew think about who might watch her if she just *happened* to leave the drapes open one night....

And that's when Drew did it. Maybe the fact that she had just gulped the remainder of the wine is what gave her the guts to do it.

Or maybe she really was a slut after all.

She kept her garter belt on, but took off the bra. She loved the way the garter belt framed her broad thighs, her wide hips, and her hourglass figure, drawing attention to the wispy blonde hair on her pussy.

She wanted to peek first, but Drew told herself she shouldn't. There was such an intense, hard thrill to just opening the curtains—and if there was someone standing there watching her, she could always pull the curtains closed again like it was an honest mistake.

But there wasn't anyone. The curtains across the alley were open, but the apartment was dark. Whoever lived there had gone to bed.

But rather than closing the curtains and going to bed herself, as she knew she should do, Drew dragged her one kitchen chair over to the middle of the room, dragging the towel with her pussy-and-lube-moistened vibrator and dildo on it over with her, and sat down on the chair.

Was there someone there in the dark watching her?

"You could get arrested for this," she told herself out loud, and spread her legs.

She could feel the erotic tension flowing from her fingertips to her full breasts, her swollen nipples, her spread thighs. She could hear herself moan uncontrollably as she rubbed her wet pussy and her engorged clit. Someone was watching her. Man or woman, she didn't care. One of the lawyers from work, finally realizing what a slutty whore this third-floor secretary was. One of the dykes from the video, treated unexpectedly to a hot show while she fucked herself on her couch. One of her ex-boyfriends, suddenly realizing what a hot piece he'd lost hold of. It didn't matter. Whoever he was, he was slipping his hand into his briefs, roused from his slumber to appreciate Drew's wanton display. Whoever she was, she was slipping out of her panties, stroking her pussy, made instantly wet and dripping by the sight of Drew showing herself off. Whoever he was, he was taking his cock, now hard, out of his Jockeys and stroking it, his hand gripping tightly as he pumped his hard flesh, as his eyes roved over Drew's mostly naked body. Whoever she was, she was spreading her legs wide and fucking herself the same way Drew was fucking her own pussy, a six-inch dildo, the really thick one, working its way in and out of her as the vibrator hummed on her clit. She was going to come. She was going to come.

Whoever she was, she was transfixed by the pumping motions of Drew's hips. Whoever he was, he couldn't take his eyes off the dancing fullness of Drew's breasts. Whoever they were, they looked into Drew's bright blue eyes and wanted her, wanted her bad—wanted her in a way no boyfriend or casual sexual interest had ever wanted her, because they'd never realized what a fucking slut she was, and how much she loved it. They wanted her, the man, the woman watching her now, because Drew was as much of an exhibitionist as they wanted her to be.

God, she was coming—coming again! Drew felt the orgasm bursting through her pussy as she lifted herself up and down on the chair so she could push the thick dildo harder into her, rubbing her cervix, slapping her G-spot mercilessly, driving herself over the edge. She was coming and moaning at the top of her lungs, not caring that the window was open or even, as she finished coming, that the light had gone on across the alley.

Not even caring that the hottest guy she'd ever seen was standing there with his dick in his hand, his eyes wide, watching her. Not even caring that he came as she came, and that he couldn't take his eyes off her, even as she finished coming and ground to a halt on the tiny kitchen chair, watching him, transfixed by the sight of his hard cock spurting come onto the carpet.

He didn't look embarrassed—this bastard was shameless! He'd turned the light on so Drew could see him, so she could see how much she was turning him on.

"Oh fuck, oh fuck, oh fuck!!" said Drew to herself as she watched the guy blowing her kisses and then running for something out of sight of the window.

Drew jumped up, still mostly naked, her face flushing hot as she began to close the curtains. But the guy got back before she could shut him out, and he held up a piece of paper.

Drew couldn't help herself. She started laughing. Her face flushed an even deeper red.

It was his phone number.

She stood there looking at him and laughing for what must have been a full minute. When she was finished laughing she just smiled, looking foolishly across the alley as he held eye contact and kept nodding and pointing at the number.

Drew heard herself give a surprisingly girlish giggle.

"Thank you," she mouthed, laughing again, blushing hot. Then she blew him a kiss, pulled the curtains closed, and went to bed.

ROOM WITH A VIEW

Saskia Walker

Fiona took a gulp of her wine and put her glass down, pushing it across the rough, wooden table with a sigh. "Dammit. I am so horny." She glanced around the small village bar with a resigned expression. "And not a hint of action for miles."

I gave a wry smile. "Hiking through Brittany was meant to be good for our souls, but you're right, maybe we should have gone to Paris instead...especially if you're on a manhunt." I was teasing her. I knew Fiona couldn't go for long without a tumble. I had to admit all this fresh air and plodding was also making me crave exercise of a much more stimulating and intimate kind.

"I thought we might meet a fit and eager young farmhand who wanted a roll in the hay." She looked positively woebegone, her pretty mouth down-turned, her brown eyes sad.

I laughed. "You're just bored." I glanced over at the barman, or *"grand-père"* as he was called by the handful of occupants. It was a very small village. "*Grand-père* over there might be able to help you out."

"I'm not that desperate. Yet." She laughed, and then she glanced at the door behind me, her eyes rounding. I heard it creak open. Someone else had arrived. I watched her face for her reaction.

Her expression lit up. She leaned forward and put her elbows on the table, ruffling her fingers through her shoulder-length, curly blonde hair to restore life to it. "Oh, my prayers have been answered, a man has appeared."

I glanced around casually, brushing an imaginary piece of fluff off my shoulder. Given Fi's reaction, I was half expecting to see a bronzed god standing in the doorway. Not quite, but he was definitely worth a once-over, sexy in a sort of sleazy way— wide, cheesy grin, slicked-back hair and figure-hugging clothes. A pair of sunglasses hung from the neckline of his designer T-shirt. A stud, and most definitely a fellow tourist. I turned back. "He put a smile on your face."

"Mmm," she purred. "Now that's what I'm talking about." Just as she said it, her face fell. "Oh damn, he's got a woman with him, she's just come in behind him."

I couldn't stop myself from glancing back. The woman was scanning the bar and its occupants with a disapproving look. She was tall and glamorous—way too glamorous for this place—and looked as if she was afraid she might catch something if she sat down in here. She tucked her burgundy-dyed bob behind her ears and stepped forward on her slender heels, as if walking out onto a catwalk. An amused murmur went round the locals.

Fiona rolled her eyes. "She's gorgeous. I hate her."

"At least the locals didn't laugh at us," I commented, suddenly proud that we had been more easily accepted.

Everyone watched as the couple walked to the bar. There

didn't seem to be any pressing need to turn away. Fiona sighed deeply. She was looking at the guy's tight derriere as he leaned over the bar to give his order. "I'd like to see that butt naked."

"You're making it worse on yourself," I murmured, imagining him naked too. His asscheeks were taut, flexing inside the tight denim of his jeans. Beneath his T-shirt, the muscles of his back were subtly defined.

I turned back to Fiona when the couple picked up a carafe of wine and looked for somewhere to sit. Apart from the row of five stools at the bar—all full with locals—there were only three small tables in the place. They took the table just a few feet away from us. The woman glanced over but never acknowledged us. The guy grinned. Fiona grinned back. I smiled and nodded. The couple spoke to each other in French. Briefly. As soon as they got settled, he started kissing the woman's neck, his hands moving all over her.

"That lucky bitch, she's going to get shagged tonight," Fiona whispered under her breath.

"I agree, but that's not the worst part. Unless they're relatives of *grand-père* and his brood, which I very much doubt since they got the same dour greeting we did, they must be staying at the *gîte,* with us." The farmhouse bed-and-breakfast had three guest rooms. Marie, the owner, had told us she was expecting another party. The hands-on couple had to be the other guests.

"Oh great, I get to look at that over breakfast too." She nodded over at them. The stud had his hand under the woman's short skirt and was stroking her thigh. The woman sipped her wine, her face expressionless. "What an ice queen," Fiona added, chuckling into her drink.

What a waste, I thought, and waved at *grand-père* for another carafe of wine.

The guest rooms were located in a teetering barn, converted to provide sparse but pretty accommodation. We made it back to our attic room, up a rickety staircase that had us breathless and giggling by the time we reached the top. We were high on oxygen, wine and sexual need.

The two hard, narrow beds looked much more inviting than they did before we'd had the wine. Fiona threw herself onto the nearest one, unzipping her jeans and fighting them and her boots off as she did so. "Oh, if he were single and here right now..."

"What would you do with him?"

"First, I'd make him lick my breasts, every inch." She grabbed her breasts through her T-shirt, massaging them deeply.

I kicked my walking boots off, shucking my T-shirt over my head.

Fiona was still lost in her fantasy. "Then I'd make him go down." She thrust her hand inside her undies. A raised knuckle poking up through the soft fabric indicated that she'd headed straight for her clit.

"This isn't helping." I laughed.

"You're right," she replied, tugging her hand free. She pulled her T-shirt and undies off, clambering under the sheets with a deep sigh.

We were just getting settled down and I was about to turn off the light when we heard a door shut, footsteps, and the creaking of the staircase. Voices sounded in the room below. Then it started—loud, ecstatic moaning—the sounds of a woman in extreme pleasure.

Fiona half sat and stared across at me, her expression incredulous. "Bloody hell, the ice queen had to be a moaner, didn't she?"

I shook my head. "It's adding insult to injury."

Fiona shut her eyes, pressing her head back into her pillow.

"*Oh oui! Vite, vite,*" the voice from below shouted.

"That lucky bitch," Fiona groaned, her hand moving under her sheet, reaching between her restless thighs.

She began rubbing and heat spread through my body, part embarrassment and part red-hot arousal. "Jesus, Fi. If you have to masturbate can't you at least turn the light out first?" What with the sound effects from below, and her obvious actions, I was fast growing wet. I squeezed my thighs together. My clit felt as if it was wired to a jagged electric current, my inner flesh aching for contact. I reached for the cord and clicked off the light. I dropped back on my pillows, wishing away the lust that had taken hold of me. As I did, I became aware of a shaft of eerie light, spanning from floor to ceiling. "What the hell is that?" I sat bolt upright, clutching the sheet to my chest, thoroughly spooked.

Fi was already out of bed and tiptoeing across the floor, her naked body strangely lit by the shaft of light. "It must be a hole in the floorboards." She knelt down, blocking out the light as she moved over it. "Oh my god," she hissed, drawing back. The light beamed upward again. "Get over here. It's a knot in the wood that's fallen out. We're right over their bed and he's giving her one hell of a pussy licking."

That did it. My hormones were already in overdrive and now they were spilling over, rampant and unleashed. As I stood up, moisture ran onto my inner thighs. I clamped them shut, wriggling them together, nearly falling over as I did so. She'd all but blocked out the light, hovering over it, but I made it over to the spot and dropped to my knees beside her. She pulled back and pointed at it, one hand covering her mouth as if she was afraid she might laugh.

I peered through the hole, gasping with amazement when I caught sight of them. The ice queen was on her back, naked, her breasts jutting outward as she lay spread-eagled on the bed. Her dark nipples and red bob looked strange and vivid against her pale flesh and the white sheets. The stud was working away in between her legs, his head bobbing and his back flexing. His bare buttocks were clenching and unclenching.

"What's happening?" Fiona pushed me aside. "Oh my god. He's humping the edge of the bed."

"Shush, they'll hear you."

"What, with that din going on?"

"*Encore,*" the ice queen bellowed, panting loudly.

Fi sat back on her haunches, one hand over her mouth, giggling. The light from the upward beam lit her face. Her eyes were full of mischief. "It looks like he's about to come all over the end of the bed."

I angled in for another glimpse. She was right. He was giving the bed some serious hip thrusts with his lower body, while seeing to the woman with his hands and mouth.

Fiona was busy moving around to my right-hand side. "Look."

I glanced up. She'd pulled back the rug at the foot of her bed and revealed another shaft of light.

"You stay there," she said. "I can't see much of her, but I've got more of him over here."

That suited me fine. I liked watching her expression changing while he did the business. Besides, the way Fi was so practical and matter-of-fact about playing Peeping Tom made me want to laugh aloud. I felt so naughty. Combined with the heady flow of lust in my veins, it was doing dangerous things to me. Furtively, I pushed my hand over my mons and fingered my swollen clit. Downstairs, the ice queen was rapidly melting. Her mouth was open, her body shuddering visibly as she shifted and arched. A great juddering moan left her lips, outdoing all her previous exhortations for pitch and reverberation. The stud moved, standing, murmuring encouragement to her in a low voice. For the first time I got a glimpse of his cock, and what an eyeful it was.

"Bloody hell," Fi whispered across the floor.

"I know," I hissed back, watching as he stroked it with a sure and adoring fist.

The ice queen sat up and smiled at him. It was the first time I'd seen her smile. She rolled closer to the edge of the bed and onto her hands and knees, her bottom wiggling in the air as she lowered her head to his groin. On her lower back, she had a tribal tattoo, a dark shape etched beneath her pale skin. When she started to mouth his cock, his head dropped back and his eyes shut, his slicked-back hair finally falling free of his skull to drop to one side.

The ice queen seemed able to make a lot of noise at all times—even with her mouth full. She concentrated her actions on his cock head, tonguing it and taking it into her mouth as if that was all that would fit. Mind you, it was very large.

"Oh come on. I'd give you a much better blow job than that, big boy," Fiona said, laughing to herself. "Suck it in, ice queen."

"No, if she did that we'd get to see less of it."

"True. Hey, ice queen, don't suck it in, we wanna see it."

"Fiona!" She was drunk. So was I, but she was verging on blowing our cover.

"Oops." She put her hand over her mouth again, leaning back from her peephole and resting on her knees to quell her laughter. The beam of light showed her ample breasts bouncing as she moved. The triangle of dark blonde hair in her groin was just visible in the fall of light. Her body was outlined with darkness, her pubic hair glistening. Everywhere I looked I saw flesh and sexually alert people. And I was no exception. My nether regions were trembling with need, my hips swiveling of their own accord, ready and primed for action. Fi's hand shot to her pussy, rubbing fast as she ducked back down to look again.

What had started out as a red-hot, full-on sex show had now developed into a double-trouble, split-screen project. Overwhelmed with stimulation, I glanced from the shadowy image of Fiona masturbating and back to the scene below. My hand was now buried between my thighs, one finger shoved inside and the heel of my hand over my clit, crushing it. I was going to come at any moment.

Downstairs, the stud was wanking his shaft while the woman sucked on the head of his cock. He'd reached one hand lower, presumably to hold his balls. How I wished I could see that too. The ice queen pulled back suddenly and knelt up, walking on her knees right up against him, whispering, gesturing at his cock then squeezing her breasts in her hands. The stud wanked faster as he looked at her tits, his cock-end dark with blood and glistening wet, his moving hand aiming it right at her.

I trembled, my climax building and rolling from my center. My sex clenched, spasmed, and flooded. Hot waves of pleasure shot through my entire groin. I wavered, slid, thought I'd slip flat out and right across the floor. The hand pivoting me on the floor was damp and I fumbled for steadiness. I blinked, attempted to ground myself, and refocused on the view below, not wanting to miss the sight of him coming.

Seconds later, he let rip and shot his load, thick white ribbons of semen covering the space between them. The hand between my thighs was drenched. Just a couple of feet away, I could hear Fi sighing with pleasure.

"Jesus, that was hot," I managed to whisper to her a moment later, suddenly self-conscious about what we'd done. I'd lost it,

the intensity of the moment compelling me to watch, to enjoy
and to come.

Fiona had stood up and was staggering back to her bed, feeling her way. She gave a breathy laugh. "Yeah, and if they're
staying another night, I suggest we do too. You've got to admit,
it's the best fun we've had so far on this bloody trip."

I shook my head: she was so right. "You know, Fi, that's the
best idea I've heard all week!"

A FLASH OF GOLD

Radclyffe

feel like I'm in college again." I surveyed the common bath-room and shower facilities and shuddered. Cold tile floors, toilet stalls that undoubtedly didn't lock, and one huge cubicle with showerheads on three walls. At least the pungent bleach smell was oddly comforting.

"Well, you *are* in a college dorm, after all." Taylor dropped her equipment bag and bent over the sink, one shallow basin in a long row of them set into a stainless steel counter beneath a smudged rectangular mirror.

"I don't know why I let you talk me into coming back every summer."

"Because you love to have five days of uninterrupted cruis-ing." She splashed cold water on her face and neck. We'd been in weapons class all morning in a poorly air-conditioned gymna-sium, and we were both dripping with sweat.

"Ha. Five days of martial arts hell is more like it." Her po-sition afforded me a very nice view of her spectacular ass. It always looked good, high and firm and tight, but in her slightly baggy white cotton gi, it was downright mouthwatering. I sidled up behind her and wrapped my arms around her waist, leaned over her, and snuggled my breasts to her back and my crotch to her butt. Her hard, tough butch butt. I wiggled a little, enjoying the way it made my clit hum. "The next time we come to one of these training camps, we're staying in a hotel. I can't even find a working outlet for my hair dryer in here."

Taylor spun around in the circle of my arms and grabbed my hips, pulling me between her spread thighs. She nuzzled my neck, licking the salty streaks. "In another few hours, everyone will be too tired to notice what your hair looks like."

When she felt me stiffen, she wisely hastened to add, "And besides, baby, your hair always looks fabulous."

"Easy for you to say." I ran my fingers through her short, thick black hair. "You don't have to do anything to yours."

She laughed and tugged up the blue silk tunic top I had worn for my tai chi swords exhibition. "One of the many advantages of being butch."

"Oh yeah?" I bumped my crotch into hers and she gave an appreciative grunt. My clit had revved up to full force now. "What are the rest?"

"This, for starters," Taylor muttered as she pushed my sports bra aside and latched on to my nipple with her teeth. She tugged and sucked at the same time, and I gushed all over my thighs.

"Honey," I protested halfheartedly, "someone might come in."

She turned her face, rubbing her cheek over my breast, and grinned up at me. "Since when do you mind anyone watching?"

"There was just that *one* time out on the balcony, and she was too far away to see all that much anyway." I remembered lying on a lounge chair outside our hotel room while

Taylor fingered me to orgasm. Just when I was about to come, I looked across the courtyard into the hungry eyes of a woman who stood statue-still, staring at us. I came so hard that time I almost flew off the chair. I moaned now, a heavy feeling in my stomach, but I kept my tone light. "And truck drivers getting a three-second glimpse while you do me in the front seat of the car don't count."

"But you like thinking they can see me getting you off, don't you?"

"Maybe." I pushed my breast back into her mouth. "And you don't?"

"Mmm." Taylor worked my nipple around and palmed my other breast, squeezing and twisting gently.

"Stop it. You know that makes me need to come." I pulled on her hair. "Come on, honey. Let's go to our room."

Taylor straightened, easing her thigh between my legs. "We have another class in twenty minutes."

I cupped her crotch, dug my thumb and forefinger into soft cotton, and scored a direct hit. Her eyes went wide as I jerked her clit. "Ten minu—"

The door swung open and a woman about our age hurried in. I got a two-second snapshot image—blonde, small and trim, pretty—before she stopped dead and blurted, "Oh. God. So sorry." Then she turned around and rocketed out the door.

Taylor laughed. "Oops."

"Great." I started to move my hand from between Taylor's legs, but she slapped her palm over mine and humped her hips encouragingly.

"Do me like that a couple more times and you'll make me come."

"Really?" I nipped at her chin, then centered myself, relaxed the muscles in my forearm, and used my hips and thighs to pivot my body easily out of her grasp. "Hold that thought."

Taylor groaned and slumped against the counter. "Who ever said butches get to call all the shots?"

"I can't imagine," I said sweetly, then caught her hand and tugged her toward the door. "Time for class."

The rest of the afternoon was taken up by nonstop workouts until six thirty, when it was time for dinner in the—*surprise!*—campus cafeteria. Since summer classes hadn't started yet, the fifty of us martial arts practitioners had the place to ourselves. The scenery was way better than the food.

"I'm going to skip the evening session," I said, pushing away my plastic tray. "My legs are already stiff, and if I don't take it easy, I won't be able to train in the morning. I'm going to take a shower and go to bed."

"Good idea. I'll come with you."

Taylor stood and gallantly collected our trays and utensils and bussed them to the conveyor against the wall. I grabbed our gear bags and followed her upstairs. We stowed our bags in our room—two twin beds, *how quaint*—and headed down the deserted hall toward the showers. I flicked on the overhead lights just inside the bathroom and, blinking against the fluorescent glare, immediately shut them off. Even my eyes were tired. A few scattered security lights provided enough illumination to see by, and I started for the shower enclosure, stripping as I walked and tossing my clothes in a heap just outside the cubicle. Taylor grabbed towels from a stack by the door and followed me. The warm water felt like heaven and I sighed with gratitude as my tight muscles began to unwind. I'd forgotten how hard it was to train nonstop for hours, especially now that my crazy call schedule made it difficult for me to work out as regularly as I once had.

"Turn around," Taylor said, "and I'll wash your hair."

"I adore you," I muttered, leaning both hands against the wall. I felt Taylor's breasts slide over my back as she lathered shampoo into my hair. Her strong fingers stroked my scalp in deep, wide circles. I moaned and dropped my head back against her shoulder. "Don't stop. Ever."

Taylor laughed and wrapped one arm around my waist, scooping a handful of suds onto my breasts with the other. She massaged my chest with the same firm circles, caressing my breasts, her thumb pausing to flick each nipple as she passed. I heard her breathing pick up.

"I'm too tired, honey."

"No you're not." Taylor bit down on my earlobe, then sucked the hurt away when I protested weakly. My body was so relaxed I was afraid I might dissolve into a heap on the floor. But when she circled her index finger in my navel, my clit twitched.

"Mmm, I felt that."

"Oh yeah?" Taylor fanned her fingers between my legs. "How about that?"

"Honey, don't tease." I turned my head and bit her neck.

She hissed in a breath and rubbed her crotch over my ass. Then she slid two fingers down my cleft and circled my opening. "I'm not."

"Oh Jesus, Taylor." My cunt rolled and my thighs went soft. "Then fuck me if you're going to."

Taylor growled and pushed me up against the wall, her arm between me and the cold tiles, her fingers buried in me, her crotch humping my ass. "I'm. Gonna. Make. You. Come."

Every word was bitten off, her hand and hips thrusting in time to the harsh syllables. The water streamed over our heads and I drifted on a mist of steam, a storm gathering in the pit of my stomach. I was just starting that smooth glide to a deep come when I heard a thin cry float above Taylor's labored grunts. "What was—?"

"It's nothing," she gasped. "Oh shit, baby. I'm gonna come all over your ass."

Her hips jerked and her fingers hit that sweet spot high up inside me and I came in her hand, my eyes half closed and blurred with water. I thought I saw a flash of gold at the edge of the steam clouds, but I was too far gone to be sure.

Taylor collapsed against me, panting, and it's a good thing she did because I needed her weight to hold me up.

"God, honey," I moaned.

"Yeah."

She kissed the back of my neck and eased her fingers out, stroking my clit as she passed it by. I was still so sensitive I came a second time, twitching and swearing at her. She laughed. When I could move, I turned and kissed her.

"Did you hear anything...odd...right at the end?"

"When I was coming?" Taylor regarded me incredulously.

"Uh-huh."

She tugged the towel from the hook and draped it around my shoulders. "No, but I'm pretty sure I saw God."

The next few days passed in a blur of pain and exhilaration. We fell into bed at nine o'clock and were up at six to start all over again. Once or twice I noticed the blonde who'd walked in on us that first morning in the bathroom staring at us in the cafeteria or during the rest breaks between training sessions. I thought at first she was cruising Taylor. Most femmes and not a few butches usually do. But then I saw her sitting on the sidelines while I was performing a tai chi form and Taylor was nowhere around. I swear she was fucking me with her eyes.

On the morning of the last day I woke Taylor an hour before everyone else usually got up.

"I've had enough of group living. Want to join me for a shower?"

She rolled onto her back and stretched, the muscles in her abdomen tensing as she bowed off the bed. She always looked just like that when she came with my lips fastened around her clit. I skimmed my fingers up the inside of her naked thigh and patted her cunt.

"Of course you can always sleep an extra hour if you don't want to play."

"Fuck that," she said, jumping up.

We grabbed clean sweats, and I peeked out the door. The hallway was empty. I looked at Taylor's naked body.

"Race you."

We ran bare-assed naked down the hall and careened into the bathroom, trying to be quiet but laughing the whole way.

"We probably woke up the entire floor," I said. "Let's claim the showers before anyone else shows up."

We'd just stepped under the warm spray when I heard the hall door open. I looked at Taylor and grimaced.

"So much for our playtime."

"Says who?" Taylor whispered and pulled me to her.

Her mouth was on mine before I could utter a protest. Then her tongue was in my mouth and her hands were squeezing my ass, and my crotch was doing a thing of its own, rolling and grinding over hers. Part of my mind was listening, but heard nothing. I hoped whoever had come in was only using the john, because Taylor knew exactly how to get me lethally horny in seconds. I heard another sound, like a half-strangled cough, and this time when I saw a flash of gold out of the corner of my eye, I saw the face that went with it. I pulled my mouth away

from Taylor, who moved to kissing my throat, and stared into
the eyes of the blonde who had been watching us all week. She
was leaning against the wall just inside the shower. She was still
watching us. And she was naked.

"Honey," I murmured.

There must have been something in my voice because Taylor left off sucking on my neck and followed my gaze. No one
moved for an eternity. Then the blonde spoke.

"Please don't stop."

Taylor extended one arm and turned off the shower, then
pushed me gently back against the wall. While she lowered her
head and covered my nipple with her mouth, I kept my head
turned toward the stranger. Her gaze dropped to my breasts
and she unconsciously brushed her fingers over her own tight
nipples as Taylor kissed and sucked on mine. The blonde's face
was dreamy, her skin flushed a beautiful rose.

"Bite them," I murmured, loud enough for our audience to
hear. When Taylor did, I cried out. The pain and the pleasure
shot to my clit and I wanted to come. The blonde's breasts rose
and fell rapidly, and she had both nipples clamped between her
fingers now, tugging and tweaking them. My voice came out
sounding breathy and thick when I spoke to her. "It feels so
good. If I let her, she can make me come this way."

"Not yet," the blonde implored urgently. "Please don't come
yet."

I laughed. "I'm taking requests."

Her face contorted for a second as she swept her hand down
her belly and into the blonde strands between her thighs. So
softly I could barely hear her, she whispered, "Come in her
mouth."

My hips twitched and I was afraid I might go off just from
the needy look on her face. Taylor must have heard her too,

because she groaned and dropped to her knees. She wedged her face between my legs and lapped at my clit with long, hot strokes. Her arm was pumping between her legs and I knew that she was jerking her clit in time to the movements of her tongue.

"Go slow, honey," I keened, my clit so hard I was afraid it would burst. "You're going to make me come."

Taylor flicked at my clit, dancing her tongue under the hood. I wanted to come so bad, but I wanted something else even more. I fixed my gaze on the stranger, staring at the slender fingers sliding through the blonde delta a few feet away.

"Let me see your clit," I gasped.

With a whimper, the stranger opened herself with one hand, pressing down so that her hard, deep-ruby clit jerked upright, exposed and glistening with her juices. I felt Taylor turn her head for an instant, and then she was sucking me even harder. I rested my head against the wall. I was losing my grip on the terrible pressure building in my cunt. "I'm going to come soon."

"Me too," the blonde cried in a high, thin voice. She kept her clit visible with one hand, squeezed between two fingers like a bright shining stone, and rubbed it furiously with her other hand, pinching and tugging. "Oh, I'm going to co...me."

Taylor groaned, her hips jerking, and I flooded her mouth with hot come as my clit jumped between her lips.

When my belly stopped heaving, I smiled weakly at the blonde who had slid to a sitting position, her head lolling lazily and her hand still clamped between her thighs. I caressed Taylor's face where she rested her head against my stomach. "Get up, honey. Let's take a shower."

"Just turn the water on," Taylor murmured, her eyes half closed. "I'm good here."

I fumbled for the dial and turned it to HOT, then beckoned to the blonde. After a few seconds' hesitation, she rose unsteadily and stepped close to us.

"You sure you don't mind?" she asked softly, suddenly shy.

I shook my head. "This is one time when three is definitely *not* a crowd."

ALL EYES
ON HER

M. Christian

The city sat around her. From where she was standing, nothing but the silver squares of windows seemed to be watching. But she knew better; she could feel them sitting behind their desks, in their living rooms, in their bedrooms, in their beds, watching her.

The gravel and tar paper of the roof was hot underfoot, but she enjoyed it. It was the totality of it, the completeness of the act that made her nipples into hard knots and stoked the fire of her cunt. Wearing slippers, shoes, or anything else would've made it incomplete, would've ruined the statement: standing naked on the rooftop, letting the city watch her.

At first Cindy didn't think she could do it. It was a private thing, a crazy thing, something to lie back in a warm, soapy tub and think about—rubbing herself into a rolling orgasm. In the real world the roof was hot; the gravel hurt the bottoms of her feet; and a hard, chill wind cut over the concrete edge of the roof and blasted through her.

Despite the pains in her feet, the chill air, and the hot tar, she stood naked on the roof of her little five-story apartment building, a fire roaring in her cunt.

There, that little square: he watched her. Slowly, he got harder and harder till all of his few inches were strong and hard in his hand. He watched, smiling, happy and excited. When he came, he groaned, and got his window messy.

Cindy watched the city watching her. Looking at one silvery window in particular she lifted her right hand to her left breast and stroked the soft skin and pinched the hard nipple.

—*they watched her. Taken with her brazenness, the attitude of this obvious species of urban nymph, who could say who started it? Maybe it was Michelle who first dropped her shorts and started the kiss. But then it could've been Stacie who started it, who put her hand between them to feel her own growing arousal. Was it Michelle who dropped to her knees and started to lick Stacie's clit?*

Or was it Stacie licking Michelle?

Who came first?

Did Stacie buck against Michelle's mouth? Or did Michelle push fiercely against Stacie's face? Or did it really matter? The end certainly justified the means—

Cindy looked up at the sun. It bathed her, baked her; her skin vibrated with the heat of it, the fire it coated her with. Right hand still on left, she felt her breast, playing with the texture of it, the underlying muscle, the strong tip of her nipple. Sun on her, she moved left to right, massaging her breasts under its warm gaze.

—*sitting on their bed, she watched the woman on the rooftop across the street. The sun was almost too bright, too hot, and for a moment she thought about what she had to do: shower, get dressed, go to work. But the woman, the daring of her, the casualness of her, kept her glued to the window. She didn't seem crazy, but that's what she had to be. To stand up there in the sight of God and everyone else and rub herself like that. It turned her on something fierce. It made her horny, that's what it did. She savored the word as she pulled herself up from sitting to all fours. Her breasts pulled away from her body in this position—they strained against her body and rolled in her housedress.*

Without thinking, she put a hand down the front of her dress and cradled one of her breasts. The nipple was so hard it ached. Cautiously, she squeezed and pulled gently at it. Fire raced through her. Her legs felt like they were going to collapse. Watching the woman across the street and touching herself, it was like she was crazy, touching herself and thinking about her nipples and between her legs she could feel herself grow wet—

Her legs were tired, so Cindy lowered herself down till she squatted over the hot gravel roof. Her breasts were heavy and tight, her nipples ached to be touched and sucked. No thought. Not a one. Watching the city watching her, Cindy put a hot hand between her hot legs. Her thighs were wet, her cunt was a damp forest of blonde curls. Her lips were wet and hot. She ran a single finger from her clit to her cunt to her ass, and shivered in delight.

—bent over the chair, her ass in the air, her arms down the chair back, her knees on the seat, Betty could feel Bob's tongue playing with her cunt. He loved to eat her and god, he was good at it. She pushed herself back toward his face, trying to get his hard, strong, tongue deeper into her soaking cunt. Then he found her puckered asshole, and started to tongue around it. Christ! She felt like screaming. She needed cock now, right now in her soaking pussy; she needed to be filled, fucked; she wanted to come and come and come! Then Bob was at her clit, and the

world seemed to boil down to the points of her nipples, the glow of her ass, the wetness of her cunt, her lover's tongue, and the joy of her clit. She was so lost, so incredibly lost getting ready to come, that she almost forgot to look up, to look across the way to see what that chick on the roof was doing next—

Cindy's cunt juice ran between her fingers. She was so wet. Her cunt was soaking, her clit was a hard bead between her legs, tucked between her lips. She'd worked out a system, and it was working real good: first she'd plunge her hands deep within herself, up and deep till she could swear THERE was her G-spot. Then she'd pull out, slow and hard, pushing aside her hot, soaking lips till her fingers glided past her clit. Then she'd work it, rubbing around and around the little bead. Then back—back to her cunt, the depths of her, her hot lips, her clit, over and over again.

Sometimes she'd use both hands, pushing all her fingers into herself like some huge cock. Sometimes she'd use just one; saving the other, wet and smelling of her cunt, for the knots of her nipples, her aching breasts.

Then she came, fast and oh-so-hard, with the whole world watching.

WALLED LAKE GIRL

Tara Alton

Late at night, I was standing in the park by the lake across the street from my apartment as I smoked a cigarette. Some people would say a girl shouldn't stand out there by herself, but heck, I've lived here all my life. I even knew Walled Lake was called this because Native Americans had built a wall across the lake to divide it, but mostly the town was called "Wall-tucky" because of all the workers they called up from Kentucky in the '60s to work in the automobile plants. This was pickup-truck, flannel-shirt, beer-drinking, redneck heaven, and I fit right in. Well, most of me fit in.

After taking a last drag on my cigarette, I crushed it out and walked back across the road to my apartment complex. This wasn't the nicest place to live. The rooms were miniscule because they used to be summer weekly rentals with a kitchenette. Now people who were financially challenged like me lived here year round.

What I liked most about the complex was how the single-story, cement-block structure was nestled inside a grove of trees. A person could get up to all sorts of things behind the building and no one would have a clue.

My thing was finding out what a man named James was doing in his bedroom. He lived several doors down from me, and I'd mostly seen him at Frigate's Bar, a local rock-and-roll joint. He took my breath away with his amazingly ripped body, his shaved head, and his plentiful tattoos. Even the intense look in his eyes made my knees go weak.

Of course, I'd consulted the local rumor mill to find out what I could about him. He was an auto mechanic who smoked Salems, stuck with Jack and Coke at the bar, and ate faithfully at least three times a week at A&W.

What I had found out about him on my own was that he had to be one of the horniest motherfuckers I had ever come across. Weekend after weekend, I had watched him pick up a variety of girls at Frigate's. He wasn't stuck on a certain type of girl either. He was an equal opportunity fucker, and he was the first man I had been attracted to since I had broken up with my boyfriend six months before.

The thing that bugged me the most about him was that he would hardly ever look in my direction. Maybe it was because I hung out with Mike Miller, a local boy whose badass family had a police file as long as his forearm, but he was a dear childhood friend. The only time I ever saw James check me out was when I was slow dancing with Mike, and he never looked in my direction again.

Another reason he might not have been interested in me was because I'm known to be a bit of a gun nut. I work full-time at the gun range, but if you had a choice between serving overcooked Salisbury steak at the Beekeeper to cranky little old women or selling an extended magazine to a Glock 19 owner, which would you choose?

Seeing how he had no interest in me, like most of the men around here, and I hadn't had sex in six months, I needed to get my jollies somehow.

That was when peeping into his bedroom became part of my routine. It had started a few weeks before when I had had too much to drink and was pissed off because he was taking some other girl home and I had to go back to my bed empty handed.

My intention was just to see what he was getting up to with her, but I found myself gripped at his window, having a rocking orgasm as I watched him fuck her, this feeling of voyeuristic excitement from my early teens rushing back at me.

My buddies and I used to peep in our neighbors' windows all the time, hoping to get a glimpse of something forbidden. It was the most exciting thing I had ever done. Soon most of my friends moved on to other adrenaline rushes, like shoplifting, but the prickles of excitement from voyeurism stuck with me.

As I grew up, I found I liked showing off even better. I was always the first one to suggest skinny-dipping or making out like mad with a boyfriend in the parking lot after school so the other kids could see us. I'd even ruined a high school group photo by deciding to kiss a girl at the moment the picture was being taken.

Tonight, there was a faint glow coming from James's window and the curtain was slightly ajar. So far, I'd seen him jacking off, fucking a couple girls, and passed-out drunk on his bed. The first peek of the night was almost like the anticipation before spinning a roulette wheel.

I peered inside his bedroom. He was lying on his bed wearing only unzipped blue jeans, jacking off to girl/girl porn. Hot damn.

I sucked in my breath, feeling a chill at my neck. He had the most amazing rock-hard boner. I know it sounds like a cliché, but it was almost like a work of art the way it was shaped, and the man certainly knew how to work it. He'd done things jacking off that I'd never even seen before.

With trembling fingers, I undid my belt buckle, unzipped my jeans and slid my cool fingers down inside my underwear. I felt a hangnail catch on my skin, but I kept going.

Suddenly, James picked up the remote, maybe to speed up the action of the two blonde bitches on the screen, and it fumbled out of his fingers and spun off the bed onto the floor. He twisted around to grab it, his gaze stopping on the mirror across from him. To my horror, I saw he was looking at the reflection of the window behind him. Had he spotted me?

I gasped, jerking away from the window like it was on fire. I quickly tried to do up my jeans, my hangnail painfully catching on the zipper, and turned to get away, but like the well-oiled machine of muscle he was, James had already bolted out of his apartment and charged around the back of the building.

The moment he saw me, he looked completely flummoxed, as if I was the last person he expected to find standing there. I took the opportunity to dart around him to the front of the building, but he must have regained his composure, because I heard his footsteps coming up behind me.

I had made it past his front door when I heard him stop and clear his throat.

"Hey," he said. "You better come in."

Hesitating, I glanced over my shoulder at him. He was holding the screen door open for me. Judging by his stern expression, I didn't have much choice if I wanted to avoid making a big scene out here.

Taking a deep breath to steady my nerves, I entered his

apartment. Although I knew the bedroom by heart, I had never really seen inside his front room. The apartments came furnished, so he had almost the same decor as me. Still, I was a little surprised to see my bizarre '60s-style vinyl sofa that looked like a sleigh. Could they really have made more than one of those?

Sitting down on the sofa, the vinyl creaking, he stared at me as I hovered by the door near the television set.

"Shit, I thought you were kids or someone worse out there," he said. "What the hell are you doing looking in my window?"

I shrugged.

"Have you done it before?" he asked.

I nodded.

"Are you stalking me?"

"No," I said. "Not really."

"Then what exactly were you doing?" he demanded.

What could I say? No amount of fabrication in the world was going to make this sound reasonable. I decided to come clean.

"I was masturbating," I said. "I haven't had sex in six months and I think you're hot."

"You're dating Miller," he said.

"We're just friends," I replied.

"You were pretty cozy on the dance floor at Frigate's."

"He was comforting me," I said. "No one has gone out on a date with me since I broke up with my last boyfriend."

James narrowed his gaze at me.

"Who was your last boyfriend?" he asked.

"Scott Pickard," I said.

Just saying his name aloud was painful for me. When he had moved back to Kentucky, he hadn't asked me to go with him. He had never even said he loved me. Oh, maybe he had said he loved my ass or my tits, but never me.

James whistled through his teeth.

"I can't believe the company you keep. What's wrong with you?"

"I like tough guys," I said.

"There's such a thing as taking it too far."

"Well, you've slept with a different girl every weekend for the last two months," I retorted.

His expression turned dark. I did have a problem with being too direct sometimes.

"And I think I know why, too," I continued.

"Why's that?"

"No one has been able to satisfy you."

"Maybe I like variety. Maybe I don't like commitment. Maybe I'm a sex addict. Maybe you have no idea what is actually going on inside my head," he said.

He paused, as if gathering his thoughts. I could feel the tension radiating in the room.

"I could have you arrested," he said.

That was it. It was time to leave. I turned to grab the door handle, but James leapt up and blocked my path. Instead of grabbing the door handle, my hand accidentally brushed his crotch.

"You want it?" he asked.

To my disbelief, he unzipped his pants, got it out and forced my hand on it. For a moment, I was so shocked that I stared at him blankly, but then I realized how hot it felt in my hand. I was actually holding it. From the look in his eyes, he seemed to be expecting me to continue struggling, but I felt mesmerized and empowered to at last be holding what I had previously only seen from a distance, feeling it pulse in my hand.

Leaning slightly forward, I wet my bottom lip and let a small drop of saliva slowly fall from my mouth onto his boner. The moment the wetness hit my hand and his skin, I began stroking him. I knew exactly what he liked because I had been watching him do himself for weeks.

As I felt the fullness of it, I let my fingers run from the bottom to the top of the head, swirling them around there, before I slid back down the other side, taking in the veins and ridges. Becoming bolder, I moved my hand back up to the top, where I started making a squeezing-the-orange-for-juice motion over the top. His face wasn't betraying that I was getting to him, but his cock was rock hard and straining in my hand. Sure, it had a mind of its own. He had just been whacking off to porn moments ago and now a girl was holding his dick in her hand. Any other man would be hard, too.

In my own pants, I was throbbing like crazy. My heart was in my throat as I realized how badly I wanted him inside me. All this pent-up sexual frustration was beating at my door. All I needed to know was if I was getting inside his head, too.

Suddenly, his eyes flickered shut, his mouth opened a fraction, and his shoulders dropped an inch.

That was all the encouragement I needed. Feeling as if my inner sex demon had been released from the depths of purgatory, I pushed him across the room to the vinyl sofa and shoved him down on his back. The moment his skin hit the vinyl, I whipped open the front curtain next to me and started peeling off my clothes. Off came my coat, boots, belt, jeans, cotton hipsters and thermo top, leaving me standing there in bare bush, socks and a camisole.

I probably looked like a sex-crazed whore standing over his erection in front of the window, but I knew this was probably a onetime shot at having sex with him in a semi-exposed situation. A fuck like this might keep me going for months, and the thought of someone actually seeing us was too incredible to imagine.

There didn't need to be any foreplay. I climbed astride him and lowered myself onto his dick. I had thought that, having been so horny for so long, I would be ready, willing and able, but I had to take several deep breaths before he was all the way in. With my hands resting on his hard stomach, I studied his face as I moved myself up and down on him, controlling the depth. He still looked startled, as if he couldn't believe I was doing this, but his dick knew what I was doing.

Sitting up straight, I started rocking back and forth. Heat bloomed across my body, my bare calves squeaking on the vinyl sofa. My hands felt as if they were burning into his stomach. With the palms of my hands, I felt up his abs to the width of his ribs. There wasn't an ounce of fat.

Everything was becoming so much looser. I was able to really move now and feel the girth of him inside me. They say that fucking is a lot like riding a bike, and you never really forget how to do it, no matter how long it's been. Riding a man cowgirl style had always been my favorite position because I was in control of my movements and I was the one on display.

Still, the ride-'em-cowgirl bucking didn't get me off as much as keeping my crotch close to the base of his penis and feeling the firmness of his public bone pressing against me did.

Arching my back, I was pushing down onto him as hard as I could when I caught a glimpse of headlights playing across the wall. Someone was driving into the apartment complex.

I looked over my shoulder at the window, feeling a chill shoot straight down my back. They could park next door and see me fucking him. This time I would be the girl with James's dick buried deep inside her, not some other bar slut. I would be the girl on display, fucking the shit out of a hardass guy like him. They could see exactly what I was doing, every fucking detail. This wasn't skinny-dipping or making out like mad or kissing a girl in a photo. This was hot, motherfucking, bang-on sex on display.

Still looking out the window, imagining someone actually standing there watching us, my body a blur of motion as James was yanking my hips up and down on his dick, I reached in between my legs, felt him sliding in and out of me, and made one frantic circle on my clit. My orgasm flared up through me, my entire body lighting up. It was one fantastic, earth-shattering high that no drug could ever duplicate. Scott had never gotten me off like this.

I could feel him coming inside me, and I heard his moans echoing off the walls.

Then all was still and quiet.

I slumped forward, my hair in my face as I tried to catch my breath, my pounding heart trying to escape my ribs. I could hardly move the lower half of my body. Every moment seemed to stretch into forever. Deep inside, I never wanted to get off him.

There was the sound of a lighter. He was lighting a cigarette and I knew it was my cue to leave. I had just embarrassed myself on an epic scale. He had just seen me at my rawest, glimpsed my core. I was the small-town girl who got her rocks off thinking someone might see her fucking in a window.

Lifting my palms off his chest, the cool air rushing against them, I was shifting my weight to get off of him when I felt his hand slide across my belly to the hem of my camisole. He slipped his fingers under it. My breath caught as there was the smallest caress on my ribs. Then he peeled the delicate top off over my head.

TIGHT SPOTS

Debra Hyde

If an interviewer ever asked sex writer Delta Faragate where her ideas came from, she'd have to look the person square in the eye and admit, "Honey, I do my best thinking while sucking cock." That answer might go down just fine in the pages of *Playboy* or *Hustler* but it'd be cause for scandal in any "family" paper or periodical. But Delta wasn't fantasizing about fame or notoriety. She was busy puzzling out the topic of her next column—and voraciously working her boyfriend's meat in the process.

She had it just right, too: matching the right force of suction to his rhythmic pumping, pressing her tongue to that one spot on his dick that made him swell toward orgasm, giving him a sensual extra by cupping his balls. His breath was ragged, his moans barely escaping his lips. She knew it was only a matter of moments.

When she heard that certain firecracker gasp of his, she knew he was there, and his dick surged and shot forth the fruits of their shared labor into her waiting mouth.

After Robert came, Delta tended to his retiring tool with gentle licks. When he recovered from his explosion, he chuckled and asked, "So what'd you come up with this time?"

Robert, the dear soul of a beau, was in on her dirty little trade secret. And he loved these working meetings of hers.

Delta mumbled something unintelligible. Robert grabbed her hair, tilted her head up toward him, and reminded her, "It's impolite to talk with your mouth full. Swallow."

Swallow she did, tasting sweetness upon her tongue. *He's still drinking OJ,* she thought.

"Well," she resumed in a more polite fashion. "Think about this: with visions of long hair and love beads dancing in their heads, America's oldest boomers turn sixty this year."

She paused, rose from the floor and joined Robert on the couch.

"I want to write about one particular symbol of hippiedom and sexual liberation."

"The peace sign?" Robert posed.

"No. The VW Beetle. Pneumatic made mobile."

"Huh?"

"Remember the first time you encountered the word *pneumatic?*"

"Yeah. In an engineering class."

Delta laughed. "Okay, so my literary reference might be lost on you slide-rule types. I first saw it in a modern lit course—in *Brave New World,* where a woman's sexual value was measured by her innate "pneumatic" ability. When I think of the VW bug, pneumatic comes to mind. And pneumatic makes me think *Brave New World* and *Brave New World* reminds me of youthful freedom and discovery, coming into your own, and the no-turning-back of the sexual revolution."

"But," Robert countered, "the revolution kind of fizzled, you know."

Delta scoffed. "You think today's sixty-year-olds are hanging up their spurs? I bet lube is selling better than ever in their demographic."

Robert smiled at Delta. She had a point.

"Why not drum up some nostalgia?" she asked. "I mean, remember the backseat? What it was like to fuck in glorious and cramped abandon?"

"I remember the cramped part."

A sly smile crept across Delta's face. "Let's test-drive a Beetle. Let's do a backseat assessment."

"Too cramped. Let's try the PT Cruiser instead."

"That's a guy car. Only guys had jalopies. The Bug was a car of its time, owned and adored by all—freedom, liberation, equality! Besides, be thankful I'm not hankering for that Mini Cooper. Remember what I told you about them?"

Robert remembered. Delta's father in the Air Force had brought a Cooper back from England in the 1950s and driving it stateside brought vocal ridicule, namely "What's it going to be when it grows up?" from guys driving jalopies.

"Call the dealer," Robert relented. "I'll take time off from work."

Sometimes, it didn't pay to be a known sex writer. Often, people didn't want to see Delta coming their way—sin by association, she called it—and trying to jump-start the Volkswagen story was a case study of people fleeing in the face of Delta's notoriety. Dealers throughout the greater metro region begged off Delta's brand of automotive review. Oh sure, they wished her well and why not? They risked nothing and if her column created a buzz, they'd reap the benefits. But help her directly? No way.

The entire situation made Delta roll her eyes and shake her head in facetious disgust.

To run with her story, Delta had had to dig into the Volkswagen underground, networking her way among Beetle hobbyists to find a car geek who owned Beetles both old and new *and* had a sense of adventure. That geek turned out to be one Paul Clotsman: middle-aged, with glasses, a receding hairline, and a swallowing tic. He owned a fleet of Beetles, one for each decade of its North American existence, and he was both open- and dirty-minded. In negotiating the terms of acceptance, his only request was that he get to stand guard over his new Bug as they did the deed.

"Don't trust us?" Delta asked.

"It's not that. I'm a big fan of yours, actually." Paul swallowed three times between sentences. "Umm, I'd like to watch."

Delta rolled her eyes as Paul, having risked it all, shuffled from foot to foot, awaiting her answer. The last time something like this happened, she recalled, was at an SF convention and it involved Klingon mating practices. Then she had declined the offer, but this time, with her deadline looming, Delta didn't have time to fuss with the details. She eyed Paul and, as he squirmed under her scrutiny, she deemed him harmless compared to that wannabe Klingon.

"Done," she decided.

Paul's swallow was working overtime when he met Delta and Robert outside his garage. He pushed open one of two rolling doors and admitted his guests to his own private little heaven, a long and deep barn in which Volkswagen Beetles sat, lined up in formation.

It wasn't difficult to pick out the new Beetle among the old.

A vibrant blue, it was rounder in the front, blunt in the rear, and shaped wider overall. Paul opened the driver's-side door and Delta motioned to Robert to get in. "We might as well do this like a date out of the seventies," she said as she made her way to the passenger side and slipped in.

Robert put his seat back as far as it would go and smiled conspiratorially at Delta. She slid her seat back and returned his grin in kind. They reached for each other and started kissing. With the action underway, Paul shut the driver's door and went to a neighboring car where he sat on the hood and watched.

Robert and Delta let their kisses lead to necking and necking to groping. They shared the hurried passion of a mutual agenda and in no time, his pants were open, her skirt was hiked up, and their first complaints came in unison. Presenting herself sprawled and spread to Robert, she yelped as the door handle pressed into her back, Robert as he attempted to straddle her.

"Damn stick shift," he complained, plopping back into his seat in defeat.

"So much for a well-planned lay," Delta observed. Struggling, she returned her legs to her side of the car. "Let's try some lap action." She dove onto Robert's cock mouth-first and started working him in earnest. She licked and sucked him, teased that sweet spot that had inspired this entire lark, and bobbed along until she muttered a second "Ouch!" This time, the gearshift was against her shoulder.

How did we do it back then? she wondered, rising from Robert's prick and apologizing. He shrugged. "It wasn't quite the right angle anyway."

"Yeah," Delta agreed. "Kind of hard to give you a satisfying hummer from the side."

"Guess you need a Hummer for that," Robert quipped.

"Ha ha," Delta said in unmistakable sarcasm.

"Lean back and put your legs up," Robert suggested. "Let's see if oral works in the other direction."

As she raised one leg to the dashboard and the other to the headrest of Robert's seat, Delta felt positively porno with her strappy little red heels pointed high. She braced her hands against the floor and seat to resist placing all her weight on the door handle, and Robert angled himself to reach her rich lap of luxury with his talented tongue. She shivered as he touched her there, lapping at and circling her clit. Delta sank into the pleasure of arousal and, eyes closed, wandered through several imaginary scenes of lust before reopening them to watch her legs bounce in sync with Robert's hearty efforts.

Looking around, she spied Paul spying her. Standing now, he peered over the hood, taking an occasional drag on a cigarette.

He reminded Delta of a long-ago beau who didn't have a car. Or rather, of his best friend, who drove them around and put up with their backseat antics. Occasionally, he would park the car and they would kick him out so they could grab a hot quickie.

Paul blushed and turned away, returning to the nearby hood like a neighbor who had outstayed his welcome.

Just like her beau's friend had done. Only Delta didn't remember the high school friend peeking quite so openly at them.

Delta shifted her focus to Robert's tongue, which was moving downward to her slit and trying to pry its way in. He lapped and poked and made some headway, but again the angle wasn't right. Delta knew her chances for an orgasm were evaporating in the process.

Just as well, really. Her hands were giving out, the door handle was again against her back, and Robert's tolerance was giving out as well. Rising up from her, he stretched and straightened, then reached a hand to the back of his neck and rotated it left, right, then left again. It cracked twice, knucklelike.

"How'd we do this when we were young?" he asked, baffled.

"Backseat," Delta answered by way of an order.

They slid their seats as far forward as possible and stumbled from the front to the back. They didn't even try to go over the seats; at their age, one of them might twist an ankle—or break a hip—trying.

They settled into place and sought out the same position. Delta hiked her legs and, grinning like a Cheshire cat in heat, raised her skirt up, slowly revealing her sweet thighs and the womanly cleft between them. Robert watched as she displayed herself and, when all was in plain sight, he let out a teasing "Yummy!"

"You're all swollen down there," he remarked, placing fingers on her clit and slit, massaging them into renewed excitement. "You look like you could come."

Delta's grin waned into a sly smile. "Maybe I will if you do it right," she coaxed.

Robert took the challenge, slipped a finger into her slick depth, and unbuttoned her blouse with his other hand. He laid her breasts bare and nuzzled his way to her nipples, sucking and tonguing and nibbling her into readiness. Delta gave in to the mounting pleasures he offered her, growing aroused enough to grind against his busy hand. She clasped his head in her hands and urged him to nibble more exuberantly. Her breath quickened, matching the heat that grew between her legs, a heat so intense, it cried out for cock. Delta pulled Robert away from her tits and cooed, "Get up here and get that big prick of yours in me."

Robert struggled to lower his pants and fully free his hard length. The metallic sounds of pocket change and his belt buckle jangled as his cock came into view, bobbing eagerly. Delta grabbed it and guided it to her. She felt its tip at her slit and she rose to meet it, contorting herself as she moved. Robert grunted, not out of passion but because he couldn't decide whether to scrunch into a rounded hump or lie flat. And no matter how Delta tilted herself, they succeeded in achieving only the slightest of penetration.

The Beetle's backseat was not ergonomically designed for pelvic assignations.

"You've got to be on top," Robert finally declared, exasperated.

They Keystone-Kopped their way around each other until Robert was on his back, one leg resting on the seat, the other stretched across the floor, with Delta spread over him, her knees competing with him for whatever seat space they could claim. Again she had him by his length and, this time, she took aim. Lowering herself, she moved slowly, sinuously, drawing him into her and making him slick with her wet glee.

Robert reached for her breasts and kneaded them. "Great globes," he muttered. He tweaked a nipple here and there, adding as much sensation as possible to Delta's sensual fucking. "You look like something out of a porn movie," he claimed.

"Oh, baby," she moaned in mock dialogue. "Fuck my pussy. Fuck it." She punctuated her words with movement. "Come on, baby, ram that big cock up my hole."

Delta giggled and looked down at Robert. Fuck-addled, he could only smile while he absentmindedly worked her breasts. "You're tight," was all he could manage to say.

But his hips did push upward. His generous length and girth plumbed her depths at the pace she commanded, plunging into her and satisfying her need to be filled. Robert pulled out almost entirely, dragging her rippling labia as he did; touched her rich spots of desire and pleasure, ground about in her, stabbed her and pierced her—and fucked her good.

Delta was there, ready. Fingers to her clit, she took him fast, slamming and banging her way to orgasm. Clenching her legs to his sides, she grew rigid, held her breath, and focused entirely on the tightening, swirling sensation until it seized her and shook her and took all she had.

When she slowed—afterglow fucking, she'd call it in her column—she noticed Paul, watching. This time, she played to him, opening her blouse further and flashing him. She toyed with her nipples and licked her lips and gave him a memorable moment.

Robert, though, had other plans. He pulled himself from her, grabbed his cock and began to stroke himself. Delta slid from him and, as he pumped himself more fiercely than she had fucked him, she settled into the gully of the backseat, watching and waiting. She gathered her tits in her hands, and pressed them together. Positively porno all over again, she beckoned to Robert, "Come on, baby, give it to me right here." She leaned forward and brushed her breasts against his hand.

It was just what Robert needed. He gasped and, with swift strokes, came, his cock a fountain that gushed over Delta's tits in several powerful surges.

Soon, in repose, Robert surveyed his pro bono money shot as it dripped from the rise of Delta's breasts. "Too bad it's so cramped in here," Delta teased. "I'd love to have you lick my titties clean." Instead, she rubbed his juices into her skin, massaging her breasts so sensuously that, had Robert been a younger man, he probably would've achieved an instant, second-chance hard-on.

A knock on the passenger-side window sounded. Paul. Delta smiled as she looked up at the man's geeky, peering face. Impulsively, she shimmied over Robert and out of the backseat. She went to her host and shook his hand so vigorously that her still-exposed tits bounced and jiggled in an unabashed and retro

T&A fashion. The way she figured it, Delta owed Paul.

As she and Robert departed, Delta buttoned her blouse and gloated over her final exploit. "If that doesn't make him masturbate the minute we leave, I don't know what will."

Robert threw her a sidelong smile as they climbed into their own car and drove away. Life with Delta, he had decided long ago, would always be exciting, so much so that he'd likely wake up retired one day and discover that he had forgotten to have a midlife crisis. But, hell, who needs a red sports car and a twenty-something trophy babe when your Significant Other brought Delta's kind of work home from the office?

Field research completed, Delta hunkered down to the task of writing her column. She wrote that the pneumatic appeal of the Beetle reborn was offset by its cramped quarters. She wrote about cracking joints and fading flexibility, how the older-aged body couldn't contort the way the teen body could. She wondered if the middle-aged need for generous backseat legroom prompted some kind of subliminal or subconscious response in boomers who bought SUVs. And she pondered whether small cars were made for outdoor sex, speculating that perhaps the Brits were so into dogging now because their cars were forever small.

Delta even pondered the possibility that Volkswagen might, as more and more boomers aged, bring back its once-hip van— perhaps as a hybrid or a green machine—and if it did, she vowed to assess its shock absorbers and cargo space. Horizontally, of course.

"Don't come a-knocking!" she proclaimed out loud as she finished her column. Then she cocked her head thoughtfully and added, "Unless you're Paul."

Deadline met, Delta leaned back in her chair and considered

treating herself to a long, hearty lunch. But first she picked up a notepad, scribbled on it, and tossed it onto her desk.

Call Robert, it said.

Story ideas, Delta needed more story ideas. And a really intense brainstorming session to boot.

REPLACEMENTS

Tenille Brown

I used to smoke. I picked up the habit right after I left my old man. Smoking became my thing, that thing I did with my hands to keep them busy, to make me feel like I was doing something with my time besides sitting and wondering what the hell went wrong. It was also good for keeping my mouth busy, kept it from yapping too much to my friends about my divorce; but most importantly, it took the focus off the thing I wasn't doing and hadn't done with my mouth in three years.

But I suppose a Benson & Hedges isn't exactly a dick.

Anyhow, I started to get this cough. It came in fits and it burned my throat and made the middle of my chest ache. Nothing ever came of it, but I never even looked at a pack of smokes again after that.

The thing about habits, though, is you can't just walk away from them, not like that. That cold turkey bullshit? I don't buy it because what happens is you wind up replacing your old habit with a whole new one. You might not realize it. You might not even know what that new habit is, but you do it.

Me, I started moving things. It didn't matter what it was—could be pictures on the walls, things in the cabinet. Furniture. One Friday night I got so fidgety I changed my whole bedroom around. Moved the dresser to the opposite side. Pushed my bed up against the wall.

That got old fast. And as it turned out, lying in that bed up against the thin wall of my duplex led me to my next distraction—listening to the couple next door fuck.

They had just moved in and so far they had kept to themselves. They had the left side, I had the right. They were this young couple. They had just gotten married and she hadn't popped out any kids so I guess it was to be expected, but nothing could prepare me for the all-night fuck-a-thons those two engaged in.

I mean, they did it *all* the time. Didn't matter if it was day or night, Wednesday or Sunday, they were fucking. They fucked so much it's a wonder she could walk the few yards it took to get those baskets of laundry up the road. And somehow after all that rocking and grunting and screaming, he made it out of there to work every single day.

I didn't begrudge them the fucking. At least somebody around those parts was getting some. The thing of it was they were so loud and so into it that it got hard for me to just listen and not do anything about the chills and vibrations their action stirred up in me.

See, he was a moaner. And she gave off these little shrieks every time she came. I learned their rhythm. I knew when she was on top and when he was fucking her from behind. I knew when he had crawled down between her legs and started eating her pussy.

And then, when I just couldn't help myself anymore, I started touching myself. Down there.

I did it a lot. It took the edge off, kept me from fidgeting and thinking about going back to the smokes or moving my kitchen table into the living room or something crazy like that. What it also did was take me full circle back to the reason I had picked up all these habits in the first place.

I wasn't getting laid, plain and simple.

Of course, I could have if I wanted to. I still turned heads. Guys still slipped me their numbers when I was out pumping gas or buying groceries. And not just old farts or perverts. They were young guys. Good-looking guys. Guys who looked and talked like they could fuck me into another galaxy.

And I'd let them, I would…if I didn't know any better. If only fucking hadn't gotten so complicated. Seemed to me it was too risky all the way around and I'd just as well have no part of it.

Well, not *no* part. I was still a woman, after all, and I still remembered what it felt like, what it sounded and tasted like, and listening to those two on the other side of that wall filled the void for the time being. Then she went and got pregnant and they bought a house clear on the other side of town.

Nobody moved in over there for a while and I didn't like the other side being empty. I had begun to take comfort in knowing that someone else was there just beyond that wall. It felt like I had company, especially when their grunts and moans joined my own in the wee hours of the night.

But then I got a new neighbor. A man. And he was single. He seemed sneaky to me, though. He did all those things people do when they have something to hide. He moved in during the middle of the night and was all done by morning. He kept his blinds closed and his curtains drawn.

He never showed his face. Ever. But I knew he was over

there. I heard him bumping around every now and then and in the evenings I heard his television click on and I would hear him laughing at some show or another.

I heard him at night, too. His shower sprayed noisily and his mattress squeaked something awful when he put his weight on it. He snored too.

I got to thinking he might be a big man. And I wondered if he was handsome.

I thought about taking something over, a pie or maybe a casserole, but that was what nosy people did, and one thing I didn't do was mind other folk's business. Well, not all the time.

I knew he had to be getting lonely over there. It's different for a man, you see. When they get restless, they go out and do something about it.

I kept hoping he would bring home a woman; you know, for company. I thought maybe he'd get one of those pretty girls from around town and entertain her for a little while in front of that television or stereo of his. He played good music. Maybe they could dance.

Then after things got comfortable, he might kiss her and rub her back a little. And if she went for that, he could gently back her up against the wall and run his hand up her skirt. And me, I might be on the other side of that wall having just decided to lie down and take a little nap, but just when I closed my eyes, I'd hear something like her blouse being ripped open or his zipper being pulled down.

Maybe he would be over there scooping her breasts out of her bra and taking one into his mouth. And she would moan so hard and so deep that the wall would vibrate and I would be lying on the other side with my legs spread and my fingers inside my panties.

My nipples would harden at the sound of his voice. I would

become wet listening to his groan as she finally reached for him and freed his dick from his pants. And when I heard her back slide down the wall and her knees meet the hardwood floor, the sucking when she took him deep into her mouth, I would push my fingers deeper inside my cunt.

I would listen for the dull thud of his palms meeting the wall when his knees weakened and he came in her mouth, against her cheek, on her chest.

But it never happened and I learned to stop waiting for it.

Then one night, he came home. I heard his boots hit the floor just like normal. I heard his keys land on the table. The television switched on. Then I heard the spray of the shower.

It hadn't been a good day for me. It was one of those times when I had to sit on the couch with my legs crossed tight and my fingers tapping against the cushions because I was so antsy. I didn't want to think about what was happening in that shower; how he might look naked, his body covered in nothing but lather.

So, I picked up my stack of mail and sifted through the bills and sales ads. I stopped when I saw a plain, brown envelope with an unfamiliar name in the window, one Mr. Douglas Harvey. The address, however, was quite familiar. It was the address of my new neighbor.

I shrugged and set it aside. I figured I would slip it in his box or under the door on my way out the next morning. I wouldn't even knock. Let him hide away over there all he wanted.

Hell, he was probably doing something illegal over there. Why else would he be so sneaky, hiding inside those walls day in and day out?

But if there was someone dangerous living on the other side of that wall, I would need to know, wouldn't I? I had to be a good neighbor, didn't I?

And the more I thought about it, the more important the letter looked. He would probably want to have it right away. It could be a matter that needed attending to immediately. And if I caught Douglas in the shower, if he had to answer the door with only a towel wrapped around his waist, well then, that would be a risk I'd just have to take, wouldn't it?

I pushed my feet into my house slippers and shuffled across the porch to the other side of the house. I balled up my fist to knock, but when my knuckles made contact with the wood, the door breezed open.

I heard the blast of the shower. I heard a deep voice humming a tune I didn't recognize. I stepped inside.

Douglas's place was a masculine version of my own. The walls were painted dark blue where mine were rosy pink. We had the same stove and fridge, the same beige linoleum on the kitchen floor. And that had to mean our bathrooms were identical, didn't it? It would mean that his towels hung on the right side of the shower and the shower, well, it was encased in glass that you could see clear through if you were looking.

I laid the envelope on the counter and stepped toward the bathroom. The door was wide open. I stood just outside, the steam from the shower tickling my cheeks and chin.

Seen through the blurred glass of the shower door, Douglas was little more than a dark brown silhouette. He was tall and lean, his long legs muscular, his ass high and tight. His head was bald and I could make out a strong, wide nose and a set of full lips.

His hands coursed over his body, rubbing soap over his chest and belly, down his legs and over his hips. Then he set the bar aside and began rinsing the suds off his skin. He held his arms up above his head, rinsing beneath them. He stepped forward to let the water spray into his face.

Then his hands began exploring. They lingered below his belly, giving great care to that great vessel that hung between his legs. Douglas rubbed at the dark brown mass that hung limp until it began to awaken and spring forth. He wrapped his large hands around his cock. He pulled forward, bracing himself with one hand against the shower wall.

He turned his head slightly.

I stepped aside.

I wondered if he had seen me.

The water beat down on his skin and he again faced forward. Low grunts raked across his lips and rose above the sound of the running water. His hand jerked faster and harder. His knees began to buckle.

Douglas licked his lips.

I clasped my hands at my chest.

Douglas came in spasms, his thick, white seed spewing forth into the heavy spray of water. He pressed both hands against the shower wall, resting and gasping for breath. Then he was calm.

He turned the water off. He reached out the shower door and pulled a towel off the rack, then wiped at his face and chest.

I stood a few seconds longer, trying to recover my bearings. Then I moved quickly and quietly toward the door and slipped out.

I left a trail of clothes from the front door to my bedroom. I jumped into my bed and slipped under the covers naked. I listened to his television blasting. I heard his voice, slow and raspy now, in a relaxed laugh. I pushed my hand beneath the covers and let it slip between my legs. I thought about the way he had looked, the sounds he had made.

I made myself feel good, made my knees knock against each other, made my thighs clench tight. I made my own body twitch and turn and then, when my fingers glistened and my wrists went limp, I screamed.

There was silence on my side of the wall and his.

When had he turned off the television? Was he sleeping? Reading?

My mind quickly grew tired and my eyes heavy. I faced the wall, pulled the covers up over my shoulders and slept.

Douglas Harvey's door opened at almost the same moment as mine the next morning.

"Morning, neighbor," I said, as cool as I could manage.

He said, "Morning."

"So, you like it around here?" I smiled then, figured I'd keep it pleasant.

Douglas pondered, then answered. "It's a nice neighborhood. Safe. Quiet. You almost feel like you could sleep, shower or... anything...with your door wide open and you would be okay."

And he looked at me in such a way that it made me wonder if he knew. And if he knew, did he mind? Did he even like it?

"Yeah, it is nice," I said. I started picking at the seam of my pants.

"Thank you for bringing over my mail last night." He winked and smiled.

I cleared my throat. Fiddled a bit with my shirt. "Oh, it was no problem," I said.

I thought about asking him over for dinner or to watch a movie or something; or, since we had obviously gone far beyond the coy stage, I thought I might just invite him to skip everything and join me in bed, but I decided against it.

Listening and watching would have to suffice. That is, until it was time to break the habit and find its replacement.

THE CHANGING ROOM

Catherine Lundoff

The bride and her pack of giggling bridesmaids and relatives were finally gone. Gone with their constantly changing demands and their charge cards and their smug wedding party attitudes. Eileen looked at the piles of dresses hanging on the hooks and draped over the chairs in the changing room and groaned. She'd be straightening out crumpled tulle and lace for the next two hours at this rate. The headache the bride had already given her intensified.

She picked up the white silken sheath dress from the back of a chair and stroked the fabric, letting the pleasure of touching it work its way from her fingertips up her arms. This was one of her own designs: all lean and classic lines, insanely flattering on the right woman.

Not that the little twit was smart enough to see that even when her fiancé pointed it out more than once. It had been hard not to stare at him, harder still not to flirt. But she'd sworn that

she'd never go for another engaged guy, not after Sam. Never
again. It was just her bad luck that a guy who looked like he es-
caped from a romance novel cover and had at least half a brain
would go for someone cute and dippy. Eileen sighed.
   She couldn't resist holding the dress up under her chin and
looking at her reflection in the mirrors. Its length and cut flat-
tered her more than it did the bride and she smiled a little at the
thought. Someday when her designs started selling, she'd have
dresses like this one to call her own. No more waiting hand and
foot on the kind of woman who would go for a nightmarish me-
ringue of lace and beads and glitter that practically stood up on
its own. She shuddered every time she looked at that one.
   The sound of a throat being cleared behind her made her
whirl around. The bride to be, a Miss Barbara Kellan, was
standing behind her, one blonde brow raised in a questioning
stare. "Well, somebody's got a lot of free time." She simpered,
something like a smile twisting her full lips.
   Eileen bit back a sharp response. That damn security bell
always stopped working when it would have been most useful.
But then this was what she got for not making sure the door was
locked after they had all left. "Is there something I can help you
with, Miss Kellan?" She grabbed a hanger and started to put the
gown away but a gesture from the other woman made her stop.
   "I saw the way he looked at you. I'm not stupid, you know."
The bride's blue eyes narrowed in a glare and her fair skin
flushed as if she was going to scream or cry.
   "I don't know—" Eileen began.
   "Yes, you do. Any woman would notice him, why should
you be any different? The thing is, he doesn't usually look back,
not like that. No, just shut up for a minute. I need to know that
he's faithful; otherwise, I'm always going to wonder where he
is. I'm damned if I'll turn into my mother." A single tear leaked

from her eye and ran down her cheek but the glare that she kept
on Eileen showed no trace of weakness.

In fact, her expression suggested something else, something
Eileen couldn't read. What the hell was this about? Did the little
moron think she was hot for her fiancé? Of course she was, unfortunately. "I wish you all the best, Miss Kellan, but what does
this have to do with me?"

"I'm sending him back here to talk to you. He'll think he's
alone with you but I'll be in there, watching." She gestured at
one of the changing room curtains. "Don't worry, I'll pay you
two hundred dollars for your time. I just need to see what he
does." Her glare turned a little desperate. "You do want the
sales from my wedding, right? Do this for me and I'll send all
my friends here. You could retire on what I'll do for you. Otherwise, well, you figure it out." She placed her hands on her hips
and stared at Eileen.

Eileen's lips parted to begin telling her off but she caught the
words before they were uttered. Business had been really slow
lately and Mrs. M. had been really good about letting her try to
sell her designs. If the store went under, she'd just have to start
all over again someplace else and that meant years of work. Besides, he wasn't going to do anything. A little flirtation and that
would be the end of it. A pang went through her at the thought
but she made herself ignore it. "Well, I'll talk to your fiancé,
Miss Kellan, but I'm sure nothing will happen."

The other woman gave a brusque nod and pulled out a tiny,
expensive cell phone. "Hi, hon. Listen, I'm really busy at the
florist and I was wondering if you could go back to the dress
store and make sure that girl wrote down cream instead of white
lace." There was a brief pause, just long enough to make Eileen
regret the whole thing.

The bride to be made it worse. "No, I don't think I should

just call. You, of all people, know what retail help is like these days. Make her show you the order. Uh-huh. Love you too, sweetie." She blew an air kiss at the phone before she switched it off. "There. Now he's on his way. Just look cute and don't tell him I'm here." With that, she turned on her heel and vanished behind the curtains of one of the other rooms, leaving Eileen staring after her.

She thought about throwing the other woman out but that wouldn't do anything except her pride any good. What was Kellan's problem anyway? The guy was marrying her, wasn't he? Still, Eileen was mad enough to flirt back now. Might as well show him what he'd be missing, marrying someone like that. Her eyes narrowed as she studied the gown.

"I'd love to see you model it." She spun around, her heart racing. The once and future groom, lone stud in a herd of fillies, was back. He lounged against the doorway, watching her from under half-closed lids. A small smile twisted his lips, making her blush a rosy pink as she hurried to hang the dress up.

She tried not to sigh and made sure she didn't meet his sharp blue eyes when she turned around. No point in giving his paranoid girlfriend something else to freak out about. "What can I do for you, Mr. Crawford? Did Miss Kellan forget something?"

"As a matter of fact, she did. She wanted to make sure that the lace on that delightful monstrosity that she insists on wearing is cream and not white."

His voice was filled with a slightly mocking contempt. Eileen managed not to smirk. "Certainly. I'll add a note to the order. Is there anything else?"

"Oh, I think there might be. She was wondering if that dress you were holding when I came in might suit the bridesmaids a bit better than what they picked. Would you mind trying it on for me? I know it's a nuisance but I'm certainly good for any extra charges you need to tack on." He sat down in the plush red chair in a way that suggested that he was staying put. His gaze wandered up her body, sending a hot flash through her like an electric shock. Uh-oh. No bad boy should be that handsome. It wasn't fair. She remembered her audience and tried to sound crisp and professional. "Do you really think that's a good idea, Mr. Crawford? Maybe it would be better to wait until your fiancée and her bridesmaids can come back to look at the gowns again. I'd hate it if Miss Kellan wasn't happy with her choices."

"Somehow I doubt that. Besides, my fiancée trusts my judgment implicitly. Relationships are built on trust like that, don't you agree? Particularly since my family is footing the bill for this whole fiasco. Old money talks, Ms. Anderson. Now, I realize you still have a lot of work to do so perhaps we should get started." His voice lost the lazy seductive quality she'd detected when he first came in and took on a commanding tone.

Eileen bit her lip, grabbed the dress and walked into an empty changing room. She yanked the curtains closed behind her, which meant the jerk couldn't see her lips move while she swore at him. Who'd he think he was anyway? Who did either of them think they were, for that matter? "Old money talks!" Give a guy a department store chain and it went right to his head.

That wasn't all it went to. Against her better judgment, she imagined him going down on her, imagined taking in his full hard length while his fiancée watched. Imagined the kind of hell he'd catch later if the bride to be watched him seduce the bridal-shop girl. Revenge might be sweet at that. She smiled at herself in the mirror. All right, he and his little bride wanted a show, they'd get a show.

She unbuttoned her neat blue blouse and slipped out of her skirt, dropping them both over the back of the chair. She studied her reflection for a moment, considering. Her bra would show at the shoulders and the back with the dress's halter neckline. After a moment's hesitation, she tugged it off. She gave her reflection a tight-lipped smile. Let him drool all he wanted.

The dress clung to her like a second skin, the silky fabric caressing her bare breasts until her nipples showed hard under it. The skirt had a long slit in it that ran from the floor to her upper thigh and she stretched her leg out to see how it looked. It was definitely too tight. And too low cut. She'd be lucky if she didn't fall out while she was parading around in front of this clown. And his little girlfriend. To top it off, she had a visible line of elastic around her waist where her panty hose showed through the thin fabric. Great.

She spun around to look at it a few more times. It did really ruin the line of the dress. Slowly she pulled the skirt up and tugged her panty hose and her underwear off. She plucked a few curls loose from the demure bun that restrained her long brown hair and gave herself one last once-over. It was pretty clear that she wasn't wearing a bra and now that the first flush of annoyance was gone, she was a little more self-conscious. Maybe this wasn't such a good idea. The bride might report her to Mrs. M., after all. His voice drifted through the curtains, interrupting her thoughts. "Still awake in there, Ms. Anderson?"

Damn him! She yanked the curtains back and stalked out as forcefully as the dress's tight skirt would permit. "Is this what you had in mind, Mr. Crawford?" Deliberately, she twisted right, then left, while she watched his reaction.

The smile was back along with the purr in his voice. "Turn all the way around if you please, Ms. Anderson. Oh yes, this is exactly what I had in mind." He uncoiled from the chair and paced around her in a tight circle, first one way, then the next. The silence between them grew until she thought she'd scream.

He took a step closer and her breath caught in her throat. Wasn't white what they dressed sacrificial virgins in? This was so wrong. The Kellan woman was going to freak. She dropped her eyes to the carpet and wondered how to get out of this. "It doesn't really hang right on me, of course. If Miss Kellan would like this dress for the bridesmaids, we'd have to do some new measurements."

"Who's the designer? I don't see a name on the tag." He reached out and caught the sales tag that dangled from the back of the dress, his fingers just barely brushing her exposed skin.

She trembled, a tiny gasp escaping her lips as a single drop of moisture worked its slow way down her thigh. *Stop it* she told herself sternly. It didn't matter what her body wanted; her brain knew better. She tried to remember that the other woman was watching, that this could cost her her job. She took in a deep breath and looked up. "It's by someone new. She's local, not very well known."

He met her eyes and his smile got a bit more real. "I think she will be. I also think it hangs very well on you. Very well indeed. May I check to see what the fabric feels like?" He reached out at her mute nod and ran his fingers down part of the skirt. This time, she couldn't bite back her gasp. His touch was like pure electricity, burning its way through the dress and up her thighs. She closed her eyes, willing herself not to want him, willing away the aching space inside her that clamored for more of his touch, more of his body than was safe to even think about. Somehow, thinking about the fiancée behind the curtain made it worse.

His fingers trailed down the skirt, rolling the fabric gently between his fingertips. She was wet now, her thighs slick with want. She fretted that he'd be able to see the skirt getting damp. Or smell her. She was nothing but longing and pheromones now, how could he miss it? He circled around behind her, still running his fingers over the skirt. The silken fabric rustled slightly, barely louder than the thumping of her heart.

"Would you like to see another dress?" She forced the words out, breaking the spell, and made herself meet his eyes in the mirror.

"I'm enjoying looking at this one quite a bit right now. Perhaps later." He tugged gently at the skirt and the slit fell open, exposing her leg up to her moist thigh. "Do stop me if I'm becoming too forward, Ms. Anderson. I wouldn't want my attentions to be misinterpreted." He murmured the words, so close to her now that the curls around her ear moved with his breath.

For a single wild instant, she wondered if he knew he had an audience. There was something so staged, so practiced about his approach that it almost felt like he was doing it for someone else. Even so, she imagined him inside her, his solid length thrusting into her until it filled that persistent ache. She could almost feel his tongue on her clit, expertly coaxing her into orgasm after orgasm.

Then she could picture him walking out the door, headed off to marry his little bride without a second thought. Just like Sam did to her. She met his eyes in the mirror again, steel in her voice. "Of course, Mr. Crawford. Perhaps you'd like to try on the tux and cummerbund that you picked out earlier to see how it sets off the dress in the bridal party?" She gave his reflection a tiger's smile. She would feel the fabric against his skin, run her fingers over the jacket's drape and watch him in the mirror until he hardened into an ache that no amount of jerking off would cure.

His fingers caressed the edge of the gown where it met the small of her back. "Certainly, if you think that's a good idea."

"Oh, I do, Mr. Crawford. I always think that you should be very sure before investing in wedding clothes."

"I see your point, Ms. Anderson. I like to be certain about

these things too." His fingertips barely touched her skin as they traced the line of the dress over the small of her back. She shifted so that the slit in the skirt fell open again and her leg was bared. His breath caught a little and her smile broadened. "You don't mind wearing the dress for a few more moments, do you?" His hand slid over her ass, touching her so lightly that it seemed almost accidental.

"Not at all, Mr. Crawford. We want you to be happy with all your purchases from Macgregor's Bridal." She ran one fingertip around the gown's plunging neckline and watched his eyes follow it as she pulled it even lower. She thought about licking her lips, running her pink tongue extravagantly over her lipstick until he crumbled. But not yet. With a careless, bright smile she walked over to retrieve the tux from the rack where she'd hung it earlier.

Once he was out of sight behind the curtains, she hesitated a moment. If she gave in to her desires, it would mean nothing but trouble. Her thighs rubbed together and she couldn't help slipping her hand up between them. Her clit burned as she caressed it, this time imagining Barbara Kellan watching her fuck her fiancé. Imagining the little plump blonde rubbing herself off in a twisted mix of lust and fury. Maybe she was even getting off watching Eileen now. She bit back a moan at the picture in her mind.

Then the curtains parted behind her and he walked in. She jerked her hand away, but not quite fast enough. He raised one eyebrow and his lips twisted. "Would you mind staying in here while I change? I suspect I'll need some help with the tie." His smile was feral, the wolf looking at Little Red. His fingers were already at his collar, shedding his tie, his jacket.

Eileen chewed her lip and made herself pace casually over to the chair and sit down. She crossed her legs so the skirt fell away on either side of her bare thigh. He followed her, shirt unbuttoned to expose broad muscles. He leaned over her and trailed one hand up her thigh. "It's your design, isn't it?"

She nodded, not trusting her voice, and found that she was running her hands over his chest. He grabbed her hand and kissed it hard, thin lips burning on her skin until she almost forgot about their audience. Then she was on her feet and in his arms, kissing him with a passion she hardly recognized. His thigh parted hers through the skirt's slit and she rocked against him, need conquering sense as her body sang to his touch.

His lips were on her neck, his teeth nibbling her collarbone as he sent one hand under the skirt between her thighs. She moaned as his fingers found their way inside her. He laughed then, a deep quiet chuckle that made her stiffen a little even as her knees melted. Sam thought his seductions were one big joke too. But then his fiancée had never come along to watch.

She pulled up his face and kissed him, savoring his taste: mint with a slight tang of good scotch. Now it was time for her lips to explore his neck and chest. To plant a tiny lipstick kiss on the white fabric of his shirt where the collar would cover it. It was a little thing, one that only another woman would notice when she kissed him.

She smiled a little then and let him spin her in his arms so they faced the mirrors together. He wrapped one arm around her, his hand finding her breast under the gown's silk and kneading it like dough. His other hand was between her thighs, his fingers on her clit as if he had always known exactly how to touch her. Her hair fell down around her shoulders, pins flying as she put her hands behind her to stroke him, to feel his hardened flesh beneath the soft fabric of his pants.

Was that a gasp she heard from behind the curtain? It definitely moved, shifting as though someone behind it was trying to find a more comfortable position. For the briefest of moments, she could see a bare leg, as if the Kellan had raised her own skirts.

He pinched her nipple unbearably hard at the same moment that his fingers bore down on her clit. There, now she was sure she heard the fiancée moan. The wantonness, the very wrongness of it excited her even more and she stiffened against him, her orgasm shaking her until she thought her knees would buckle under her.

He lowered her to the floor then, eager hands pulling the dress up and fumbling at his belt. She sat up, her lips on his skin as she unbuckled his belt and unzipped his fly. He was hard and eager in her hands and she lowered her mouth to run her tongue against him, laughing softly when he groaned. There was a soft crackle as he pulled a condom from his pocket and she forced herself not to grimace. Of course, he'd be prepared. You never know when a woman might give herself to you, wet, hot and eager.

But the ache inside her didn't care about her pride. She pulled the package from his fingers and opened it with her teeth. He gasped for breath as she rolled the condom over his penis, stiffening more as she touched him, his hands ruthlessly crushing the fabric of the gown up around her thighs. The carpet was rough against her bare skin as he drove himself inside her and she wrapped her arms around his neck and welcomed his tongue in her mouth, spreading her thighs to take him in.

He twisted so that his fingers found her clit as he thrust against her, sending little shocks through her. She wrapped her legs around his thighs and tried to pull him further inside her, arching her back a little. He dropped onto her then, his hands on her shoulders gripping hard enough to bruise. She thrust back against him, moaning a little. He was muttering things in her ear, something about how hot she was, when she stopped his mouth with her own.

She imagined what it was like between him and Barbara when they were doing this. Did he want her the same way? Did he take her the moment that she craved him? Was anyone else watching when they did it? Her thighs and the carpet beneath them were soaked at the thought. For a moment, she even thought about calling out to Barbara, picturing those rounded lips on her nipple while the other woman's fiancée thrust his way into her. She came then, bucking under him in wild desire.

His mouth was savage against her lips, her neck, her shoulders. The dress would never be the same, she thought distantly as his hands crushed the fabric beyond repair. She groaned at the pain of the realization and the pleasure of him inside her rolled into one. He came then as though her small sound had given him permission. He even gave a small shout, just loud enough to mask the sound of the bell by the door, as Eileen realized a moment later.

"Charlie? Are you still here? Anybody around?" Barbara must've gone over to open the door. *This should be interesting.*

"Shit!" Crawford pulled out of Eileen, swearing softly. His erection plummeted as he yanked off the condom and zipped his pants up. "Can you get out into the other changing room?" he whispered to Eileen, eyes wide and somewhat panicked as he leaned down to help her up.

It was quite the act. It might even be real. Eileen gave him a considering look and trailed her fingers over his crotch, smiling when he stiffened a little under the pressure. "Sure thing, lover. But what's in it for me?" It would be only moments before his bride began checking the changing rooms; she could see he knew it too.

"Shit! What do you want? Money?" He pulled his wallet

from his pants and she reached out to hold his hand in place.

"I'm not a hooker so don't bother giving me a twenty or two. Your family owns Crawford's department stores, doesn't it?"

Light dawned swiftly. "You want the stores to carry your designs? I can't guarantee it but I can get you an interview with the top buyers, with my recommendation. Please..." His eyes were desperate now, darting to the curtains until she almost laughed.

"Good enough, Mr. Crawford. I look forward to hearing from you so that nobody else hears about this. Understand?" She paced out between the curtains into the next room, casting one backward glance to make sure he watched the graceful swing of her ass walking away. She smiled at her reflection as she heard his fiancée open the changing room curtains behind her.

"There you are! What are you doing here, Charles? Where's that girl who's supposed to be waiting on us? I called and called." Charles mumbled something inaudible and Eileen grinned to herself as she shed the gown and pulled on her regular clothes with an easy grace.

Clearly Charles's betrothed was going to pretend nothing had happened. She decided she'd play along a bit further and yanked all the remaining pins from her hair so that it tumbled to her shoulders. Then she bit her lower lip to make it blush pink. She gave herself a critical look to make sure she appeared tousled enough and slipped through the curtains toward the back room. A few seconds later, she emerged carrying a box with a new tux in it.

"Oh, Miss Kellan! I'm sorry I didn't hear you come in. Is there anything I can help you with?"

The other woman's eyes narrowed but Eileen couldn't help noticing that she looked pretty tousled herself. "Shouldn't somebody be watching the counter in this place? I wouldn't want my dress getting stolen." Her gaze darted from her fiancé to Eileen, almost making the latter smile. Charles looked nervous, one finger tugging at his damp collar as he disappeared to go change.

"You going to tell him?" Eileen smiled cynically.

"There's nothing for me to tell him. Or you either." Barbara Kellan pulled a debit card from her purse and held it out. "Two hundred dollars. Take it off this. And give me some of your business cards." Their fingers touched as Eileen reached automatically for the card.

A shock went up her arm. "You knew what he'd do, didn't you? So what happens now?"

Barbara's lips thinned into an almost smile. "We'll be back, of course. I think I do like that gown you were showing us earlier better than the one we picked for the bridesmaids. I guess we'll just have to do more fittings for the whole party. And it'll be our little secret. Guilt sex is always the best, don't you think?"

Charles walked in and gave them both a slightly nervous stare. A few moments later the happy couple were on their way out. He didn't risk a backward glance but she did, and Eileen composed her face into an expression of polite interest. She wondered how long it would take before he figured it out, and what his little bride would get out of him before he realized he was being played. Relationships were built on trust, indeed. Her lips curled in a wry smile as she locked the door behind them.

MY FINEST HOUR

Stan Kent

There's a line in an old Blondie song that gives me an instant hard-on, and not just because it's Debbie Harry that's purring the words. The song is "Picture This," and in it the delectable Debbie offers her lover her finest hour, the one she spent watching him shower.

Now there's a dedicated voyeur's manifesto. In those few words Debbie Harry sums up my libido to a tee. I'm a watcher. I'm way more of a watcher than stuffy Rupert Giles ever was with Buffy. I get off watching my girlfriend do everything from scratching her butt as she stumbles to the bathroom half asleep to take her morning pee, to trying on shoes, to having sex—with or without me. Gym time is another gawk fest; I especially enjoy watching her get all sweaty in her skintight sexercise clothes. But the prime time on my sneak peeks channel belongs to watching my girlfriend shower, and Lizzie loves taking long showers. Just like it was for Debbie, these are my finest hours. Lizzie so likes putting on a watery show I often wonder if she isn't a closet X-rated water-ballet wannabe.

Notice how the word *shower* contains *show*. Show and shower—the two go together like a wet pussy and a stiff cock. Our glassed enclosure is her stage, and I am her rapt audience in my sunken tub catbird seat, ogling her shower show while I jerk off in the warm womb of the bath's oily water. It's my luxurious private and personal peep show that satisfies my fundamental sexual need to watch my lover engaged in what would be private and personal moments if it weren't for the fact that I'm watching. I've always enjoyed the thrill that comes from a sneaked peek. One of my earliest sexual memories came when I was seven, in primary school in England. I accidentally dropped my pencil, bent under the desk to pick it up and saw right up my teacher's skirt to her stocking tops and garter belt. I dropped my pencil a lot after that and have been a confirmed voyeur ever since.

Lizzie understands my need and indulges it, and has done so from the very beginning of our relationship. I've always enjoyed watching her shower, even when we lived and fucked in a cramped one-bedroom, one-tiny-bathroom apartment, and I had to sit on the toilet to watch her do her thing through that hideous but tantalizing dimpled glass. When we moved on up and were house shopping we always rushed to the main bathroom first, no matter how gorgeous the canyon or city views were. The voyeur's dream layout of our current master bathroom was what sold us on this house in the Hollywood Hills. Whoever did this remodel was a kindred spirit. The bathroom is floor-to-ceiling slate with candleholders built in. Skylights let in sunlight and moonlight. The tub is a huge sunken Jacuzzi oval big enough for four people to have sex in—easy. The shower is a floor-to-almost-the-ceiling curved glass enclosure at the foot of the tub. I can and do imagine what went on before we took over.

Lizzie and I are what you call a modern couple. We're in a committed, long-term relationship but we're not into monogamy. We play around, always together and always safely. It turns me on to watch her with another man or woman, but even though I'm a dedicated voyeur, my watching is usually a prelude to doing. Good watching is foreplay, building up the anticipation as an invitation to participation. After Lizzie's been lost between someone's thighs, and her legs are spread, and I've watched her writhe and heard her come, I enjoy joining in the crush of bodies so I can fuck Lizzie in her sensitized sexed-up state. It's such a thrill for us both to find each other after we've begun our intimate contact among an anonymous collection of entwined bodies. She's done the same to me after I've been lying on my back, some tasty morsel sitting across my face. I'm eating pussy, and I feel those signature lips on my cock, and I know it is Lizzie settling her cunt onto me while she kisses the woman whose pussy I'm eating. I know it is Lizzie not just because I know how her pussy feels but because I've seen the photos and the videos.

Yeah, I love to watch, and she likes to show off, and this particular night had been a fabulous feast for *les yeux*. We'd hosted one of our regular parties for like-minded modern friends and selected newbies. Lizzie had been in a fine flirtatious spirit. She'd wasted no cocktail and nibbles time before bedding a guy she'd had her eye on for quite some time. She'd taken him upstairs to a candlelit bedroom, and I followed and watched her fuck him from the balcony while some bright soft thing he'd come with sucked me off. The moon reflected on the girl's pale cheeks and on Lizzie's ass as she moved up and down on her conquest. It was a wickedly magical synchronicity. Feeling the tight sucking on my cock as I looked from the girl to Lizzie's ass as she bounced up and down made me feel like I was fucking Lizzie in the ass. Such are the pleasures of being a voyeur with a voracious imagination. Transference is easy.

By the time we came downstairs there were people fucking everywhere. The place was an ecstasy-fueled pleasure dome in more ways than one. Everyone was rolling from encounter to encounter. It was sexual and primal, hot and amazing, and through it all I kept my voyeur's eye on Lizzie as she flirted and fucked. My eye, even if it was just the littlest bit of a corner looking over some hottie's shoulder as I kissed her, was never far from clocking Lizzie's every move. The woman is amazing in the way she always seems to be doing something to turn me on, even from far across the room. Her pull on me is as pervasive as the sun's tug on the planets. I orbit her space, forever feeling the universal, undeniable force of her attraction. We are made for each other. Our sexual peccadilloes yin and yang together. It's a match made in Freud's heaven.

It was about four in the morning after some six hours of non-stop sex when the party started to wind down. Some people had passed out so we let them sleep it off on the floor. A few of our close friends settled into the spare bedrooms. Some people took taxis home. Others had designated drivers. Some were still going at it; just like Leonard Cohen, we don't let anyone go home with a hard-on.

Lizzie was kissing a couple good night while stroking their still-naked genitals. She'd enjoyed a debauched threesome with them that had added a few more entries to the Kama Sutra. I whispered into her ear that I was going to take a bath to clean off all the various bodily fluids I'd accumulated on my skin. She said she'd join me soon, and I knew what that meant. After all the sex with other people and our own share of fucking each other she was flying high and not ready to come down, so she was going to give me a special shower show. Even after all that actual fucking my heart raced and my erection returned at the prospect of watching Lizzie dish out her special blend of sex and showering. I followed my hard-on upstairs and ran a gorgeously hot full tub and added some Hells Belles oils to give the water just the right slippery consistency for maximum-pleasure masturbation. I lit candles and turned off all the lights and settled into the elixir, making sure I had a good view of the shower through the steam and candlelight.

It felt good to wash the sex from my skin. As much as I enjoyed our flings, I enjoyed our time together even more afterward. All that public fucking was foreplay for our private fucking, and it was always supercharged after ecstasy-fueled nights like the one we'd just enjoyed. It was our way of staving off the coming down, and getting cleaned up in our special way was our transition from sharing our sex with others to focusing on the love and lust that was purely ours. We've come to appreciate that so much of the enjoyment of sex with other people is in the recounting. Like Chinese or Italian food, sex is better reheated. Hearing Lizzie tell me while we fucked what she thought of some guy's cock, or how he kissed, or how tight some girl's pussy was and how it tasted adds another pleasure dimension to my voyeurism. I'm convinced it's why I became a smut writer. Transcribing the sex I've watched is in many ways as much of a pleasure as watching it, and Lizzie always gives me so much grist for my sexual mill.

I was gulping down the necessary bottles of cold water when Lizzie came into the bathroom. She blew me a kiss and slipped out of the slip top she'd worn off and on throughout the evening. She turned on the shower and stepped inside.

Showtime...

It begins with Lizzie putting her face into the hot water stream. She is five-and-a-bit feet of sex on legs so she's the perfect height to angle her face upward a little, like she does when she kisses me. Under the shower, the pulsating rain kisses her face and drips down, exploring all those lovely curves on its delightful journey down to the drain. If I were shower water, this is how I would want to go to that big sewer under the ground. Those water drops are lucky. What a joyous journey they have from the moment they spurt from the showerhead, hitting Lizzie's forehead, trickling down over her closed eyelids, channeling either side of her nose, kissing her lips, where, if they're lucky, a few might get swallowed to make it out the other side of her delectable body when Lizzie pees. The survivors cascade over her chin to trickle down her neck, following the path that I especially like to nibble on that leads to those pert and petite tits with nipples that never seem soft.

I'm convinced empathy is an essential element of my voyeurism. It's not just watching. It's watching someone or something go where I have boldly gone before. I know how good that someone or something must feel enjoying Lizzie enjoying herself, and that makes me feel good, like I have seen something beautiful unfold. Even though I am just watching, I have, in some causal Karmic way, orchestrated the ecstasy and made the Universe a better, sexier place.

Those water drops ought to thank me, the lucky little buggers. I watch them carom over the curves of Lizzie's breasts and nipples, zooming down to that slight convexity of her lower belly where they often pool in her strip of light brown pubic hair before the lucky ones trickle over her pussy, and the less bold just leap off to plummet to the shower floor or ski down her thighs and calves and angelic ankles to wallow around her feet. I know all this because I have been there, done that. My tongue has been everywhere those lucky water drops have, and that, as I have alluded to, is the key to my voyeurism. Maybe some voyeurs who are more on the Peeping Tom side of things can get off watching anonymous people, but for me, my ogling has to be personal.

So far all Lizzie has done to excite me is stand in the stream and angle her head upward to get wet. Me, I've been stroking my cock under the oil-infused water, lost in the finest hour of Lizzie's body being revealed in the chiaroscuro of our candle-light- and steam-filled bathroom. Watching Lizzie like this feels like when I'm inside her. I feel my cock working inside her cunt as I stroke myself. In my bath, watching Lizzie, it's like I'm immersed in her enfolding, dripping wet, luxurious pussy.

The fun really starts when Lizzie begins to soap herself clean. That's when she stretches one arm upward as the other soaps underneath, emphasizing her tiny waist. Then she alternates and spins to rinse off and every delightful muscle tenses. It's like she's dancing naked in the hot summer rain. Then she stops, and her ass is facing me, and she pauses. The lower curve of her butt draws attention to the slight separation of her legs, and in the flickering candlelight, through that shadowy space between her thighs, I see the drenched tufts of her silhouetted pubic hair. She parts her legs further and pees, and I see the trickle join the shower water. After a little sigh of relief, she soaps her cunt and ass and cleans every little fold that has captured so much pleasure tonight.

Next she bends to soap her legs and her long, drenched hair drapes to her feet. She's bent over so she shows me the heart-shaped curve of her ass and the winking pout of her pussy, not now obscured by shadows, and it's all I can do to stay the voyeur. Faced with such an inviting sight, I want to be the doer. I want to get out of the tub, go dripping all over the floor and enter the shower and fuck Lizzie into tomorrow. In previous shower shows I've come many times by now, but tonight, after so many orgasms leading up to this moment I'm Tantric by necessity and desire. To come right now would spoil the shower for it is in no way over. This is my finest hour and I'm going to enjoy every sexy second of it. I have so much to look forward to. She's going to wash her hair and when she does, her breasts will move up and down with every massaging of the shampoo and conditioner. Then she'll wash her bush and pussy again, and it will look like she's playing with herself. Finally, she'll soap her ass, making sure she's clean for later when I'll rim her.

She does all this and I watch, and no matter how many times I watch her go through these motions, they never get old. They keep me and our romance young. Every time she showers it's like I'm seeing her revealed naked for the first time.

Now that's she's soaped clean she'll start to relax under the water, putting on more of a show. She lets the heated stream soothe her muscles. Her head rolls from side to side as the hot water eases out the kinks but not the kinky. She bends over into a stretch. I sink lower in the water to get the best low-angle view of Lizzie's ass. She's fully bent over, touching her toes. Her butt glistens from the cascading water; the candlelight flickers, revealing details like a developing photograph. From this vantage the view is unbelievably sexy, sweet and raunchy too, and my eyes drink in the puckered rosebud of her ass as it winks at me. This is the kind of peekaboo view that men in raincoats would pay lots of sticky money to see.

I am a lucky man. I don't need a raincoat; this show is free and much better than I've ever seen in any strip club or peep show around the planet.

The bathroom door opens, disturbing my enjoyment, and in comes an intruder. It's a guy. I vaguely recognize him as one of the newbies. He's wearing a suit and tie—something expensive and black—probably Dior. He's tall and his hair is longish and black. I'm not sure which woman he was with. He seems out of it. I'm about to tell him that this is a private show, that the guest bathroom is downstairs, but I hesitate. I'm a voyeur and these little accidental moments are what I live for. They give me a god-like feeling of watching mortals at play.

He doesn't pay any attention to Lizzie, she doesn't notice him, and he can't see me in the tub. I hold my breath just to make sure I don't shock him out of his trance. He makes his way over to the toilet, takes out his cock and pisses. It's a long piss from a big cock, and I hold my breath all the way through it. I don't want to disturb him. I want to see what happens once one need of his cock is taken care of. My heart pounds, and I feel the pulse in my cock as I squeeze the shaft, the head engorging.

Obviously relieved, he leaves his cock out after flicking off the last few drops, and he moves to the sink and washes his hands. He splashes water on his face, and as he looks up to the mirror he sees Lizzie in the shower, and yeah, his cock stiffens from the sight of Lizzie bent over. He watches her perform her show for me, and he strokes his erection into a hefty fullness I know Lizzie will enjoy. My finest hour just got a whole lot finer. I'm watching them both do their thing—Lizzie showering and her intruder watching and wanking—and I'm stroking my cock.

He walks over to the shower, opens the door and steps in, fully clothed, cock out. Lizzie is startled. I think at first she thought the guy was me, but she quickly realizes the differences and straightens. She looks in my direction with that what-shall-I-do? look that really is more of an I-know-what-I-want-to-do-but-should-I? request for approval. This is my finest hour, our private time, the party is technically over, and it is nice of her to be so considerate. I smile and blow her a kiss to let Lizzie know that whatever she wants to do is okay with me. She blows me back a kiss and makes no attempt to repel her bespoke intruder. Our sex party continues in my finest hour. Picture this: he's fully clothed and getting wet. Lizzie is naked and drenched. He pulls her to him and they kiss. It's not a tentative hi-pleased-to-meet-you kiss, but a full-on let's-not-fool-around-with-foreplay, let's-fuck kiss. She wraps her arms around him and they kiss in the torrents. He puts his hands on her ass and lifts her to her toes, spreading her asscheeks toward me. He doesn't know I'm there, I'm sure, but he gives me a fabulous view of my girlfriend's sodden asscheeks pulled apart as her pussy grinds against him.

They continue to kiss, hands roaming and exploring. Lizzie's hand drops between their crushed-together bodies and she's stroking his cock. He pulls away from her slightly, reaches into his suit pocket while still kissing and pulls something out. He tears the package open with his fingers and slips the condom over his cock. He puts his hands on Lizzie's waist and lifts her up. She swings open her legs and wraps them around his waist. He pushes into her, pressing her against the glass. He doesn't waste time. He's into her like a steam train, and I have the seat at the end of the tunnel. It's breathtaking. In all my years of watching Lizzie I've never seen her fucked from this angle. Lizzie has strong legs and abs that come from miles and miles of biking and hours and hours in the gym and she puts them to good use doing sit-ups on his cock. She arches her back and that little motion pulls her up and he thrusts into her and she folds down with a thump that I just know is working her clit into a thundering rumble.

It's hard to believe what I'm watching is actually happening and not some ecstasy-fueled sex flashback. It's made all the more fanciful and exciting because of the dim flickering candlelight and the diffusion of the water and wet shower glass. It's extreme peekaboo, and what I don't fully discern I make up in my vivid imagination, only to have it confirmed or amplified as shapes shift and reality emerges. Picture this: she's naked and drenched. Picture this: He's fully clothed and soaked. Picture this: it's the most erotic sight I've ever seen in all my finest hours of watching Lizzie shower. Picture this: I am the cameraman of a hardcore porn vid. From the lowly vantage of my watery lens I'm transfixed by the sight of his condom-clad cock sliding in and out of Lizzie's tight pussy. Picture this: with every lunge, her ass presses tight against the shower glass, and as his cock goes in and out I actually see the grip of her pussy lips dragging along his shaft. I feel it too, because I crave that sight when we're fucking. I often look down and watch my cock going in and out of my girlfriend when we're fucking, and it's just like what I'm seeing now. Only it's not my cock because my hand grips my cock like Lizzie's pussy would, and I have to stop stroking my erection because I'm afraid I'll come and miss something in the brain-melting state of my release. Picture this: my finest hour—watching Lizzie get fucked in the shower.

By now Lizzie and her paramour have reached a noisy rhythm. Their moans and Lizzie's encouragements to fuck her hard rise over the roar of the cascading water, and now it's not just a visual show but a complete Sensurround experience, like when *we* fuck. Lizzie likes to be taken hard and loud, and this guy rises to the occasion. He's fucking her like she's a rag doll and she loves it. They haven't stopped kissing since he entered the shower, and with each slap-slap of Lizzie's ass against the shower's glass walls they're making one hell of a din. It's the noise of unabashed wet fucking, and it's the soundtrack to my visual treat. If I wasn't so captivated I might worry that the glass could shatter, but I'm not about to be bothered by such design worries right now because I saw the plans from the previous occupants. Like I said, the people who fucked in our shower before us were kindred spirits. Our shower was designed for an orgy of fucking. Lizzie and I have tested it many times. It's safe for sex of any kind, including the extreme, soaking-wet, butt-slapping-against-the-glass kind I'm voyeuring right now. No problem.

Lizzie breaks away from her fucker's kiss and throws her head back. She's laughing, and that tells me she's coming really good. When Lizzie explodes from deep inside her pussy she laughs. It's not just a little giggle; these are bring-the-house-down hysterics that have often totally sent an otherwise serious orgy into delirium. Once she starts, it's infectious. Other women laugh and come and guys fuck harder and lose control no matter how hard they were trying to last. Lizzie's orgasmic laughter is a siren song inviting all around to join her on the rocks of lustful abandon, and right now she's about fifteen on the one-to-ten out-of-control scale. She's gasping for breath and pulling herself up and down on his cock, and he's not distracted by her laughing —which is a good sign. Less-than-confident guys shrink in the face of such an unabashed outburst, but I do believe Lizzie's fucker has a smirk on his face, and he doesn't miss a beat. He keeps fucking her like he means it.

She goes limp, and he lets her slide from him. This is a treat to watch. Lizzie slides down the glass, and I see it all. Her soaked naked flesh glistens as he lets her down gently. She's sitting on the floor, legs spread wide. She's still chuckling. He's blocking her from the shower. The water's hitting his back. It's the calm before the storm. She angles her head up and reaches up for his cock. She pulls off the condom and pulls him to her. She takes his cock in her mouth and sucks, and she's still chuckling a little because the shower water is actually running down the guy's back to splash on Lizzie's sensitized pussy. Each little drop is like a tongue lashing, and I can see that's exactly what Lizzie is reciprocating with. She's pulling him into her mouth, and he's thrusting with his hips, holding on to the top of the shower for balance. I can't help myself any longer. To hell with self-control. I don't care if he knows I'm watching and wanking. This is my finest hour.

As Lizzie sucks him, I time my strokes to match her mouth's pumping. Water's flowing over the sides of the tub and onto the tiles, but Lizzie and her lover are oblivious to my antics. He's watching her suck his cock, and I can't say I begrudge him his focus. Lizzie likes to rub the cock head along the side of her cheek, massaging it with her tongue. It not only feels amazing but it looks astounding. It feels like she's tying it in knots, and I can never last very long when she really sucks down on my cock like that.

And despite a night of what was probably relentless fucking, neither can this guy. After a few precious minutes of Lizzie's finest-hour fellatio his body stiffens and he arches his back. Lizzie pulls him out as he starts to come and he shoots over her head and splatters a large stream onto the glass. I actually flinch, thinking that I might get an eyeful. And I do, from my cock, as I come too. Our moans echo. I submerge to wash away my orgasm.

When I surface, at first I think that they've left the bathroom. I don't see any bodies in the shower, so I sit up in the tub, and then I notice them. They're on the shower floor. He's eating Lizzie. With their splayed bodies blocking the drain the water builds up in the shower, but they don't mind. They're like some primeval amphibious creatures writhing in a stream, struggling for the land so they can multiply or die. He has his hands on Lizzie's hips, and he's working her on his face, and she's pressing down on his back with her legs and they're squirming around.

Lizzie wedges herself in the corner and sits up facing me. This is the first real eye contact we've enjoyed since she began fucking the sharply-dressed man, and she smiles and blows me a kiss. My cock hardens. I blow her a kiss and smile back.

It was my finest hour—the one I spent watching Lizzie get fucked in the shower—and then she beckons me over to join them, and I realize that it isn't just *my* finest hour. It's our finest hour, and picture this: it has only just begun.

THE STARS
FELL DOWN

Kristina Wright

The accidental brush of a hand. A knowing look across a room. The tilt of a head toward the door. Telltale signals shared between spouses or, in this case, between lovers whose spouses were oblivious.

Cole was drunk. It wasn't apparent in his demeanor, but I knew the signs. He brushed by me on his way through the kitchen and his hand touched my ass. He paused, standing there for a good minute and blocking the path of two other guests trying to get by. I wanted to press against his hand, but I knew better. It was too risky.

I glared at him, knowing it didn't matter. "Had too much to drink?"

"Not too much. Enough to know what I want," he said. He leaned close, stirring the hair on my neck as he whispered, "We're leaving soon. Meet me."

I didn't have a chance to say no or, rather, ask where and when, because my husband Brad came up to us just then. As if sensing that his territory had been encroached upon, he wrapped his hand around my waist and gave me a little squeeze. Cole took his hand away from my ass at about the same moment and I wondered if the two had touched in passing.

"How's everything, sweetheart?" Brad asked. He kissed me on the cheek, but he only had eyes for Cole. "Everyone seems to be having a good time."

My parties are legend. I am the hostess extraordinaire, making sure everyone has enough food, enough drink, a good time. I smiled at Brad, ignoring the hard set of Cole's jaw. "Everything's great. I think we're running low on wine, though."

"I can go get more."

I could practically feel Cole tensing, though he was no longer touching me. "Oh no," I said quickly. "We'll be fine. If not, I can run out later."

"Well, let me know if you need anything," Brad said, releasing me to make the rounds once more.

"Nice," Cole murmured. "I was starting to think you didn't want to be with me tonight."

I didn't have time to respond. Rachel, Cole's wife, appeared at his side. I wondered if she'd heard what he said. One look at her bland, expressionless face told me she hadn't.

"I need to go home," she said to Cole, ignoring me. It wasn't that she suspected anything; Rachel simply didn't like parties or people. She let Cole drag her to these get-togethers, only to stand off to the side, hardly speaking, and demand to leave shortly after arriving.

I watched as he pulled her close and brushed her hair aside to lay a kiss on her neck. I shivered, knowing what that felt like. I wanted his touch and was jealous to the core of my being that she was getting it instead of me. Cole knew what he was doing, knew that he was pushing me.

"I guess we'll be going," Cole said, sounding genuinely disappointed. "Tell Brad thanks."

I saw them to the door, hugging Rachel first, then Cole. His touch was polite, distant. His words in my ear were another matter. "The university parking lot in an hour," he breathed so softly I wouldn't have heard him if his lips hadn't been touching my ear. "I need to be inside you."

I clung to the doorknob as I closed the door behind them. Weak-kneed with desire, I had the fleeting thought of refusing his request, of simply not showing up. I checked my makeup in the mirror by the door, noting the flush in my cheeks, the way my eyes sparkled. He did this to me, so easily.

I would go. I would think of an excuse to be gone for a bit and I would leave my party to fuck my lover. I smiled at my reflection, but it didn't quite reach my eyes.

The minutes dragged on. Ever the hostess, I poured endless glasses of wine and made small talk about how Bobby was doing in Little League and whether our subdivision needed stricter covenants. Finally, I slipped away. I told my best friend Theresa to tell Brad I'd gone for wine. Theresa knew about my affair with Cole and seemed to get a vicarious thrill from hearing about my escapades.

"I won't tell him until he asks," she said. Theresa is a good friend.

It was a short drive, no more than fifteen minutes, but the lights worked against me and my frustration level was near to the breaking point when I finally pulled into the parking lot. I slowed the car, realizing I had been driving well in excess of the speed limit. I needed to see Cole and nothing, not traffic lights or speed signs or twenty-five people at my house would stop me.

Cole teaches at the university. He is a professor of philosophy and ethics, the irony of which doesn't escape him—or me.

His car was there, parked in the shadow of the arts and letters building. I saw his silhouette in the driver's seat, could see the movement of his fingers as he drummed the steering wheel. Cole is an impatient man, especially where I'm concerned. The knowledge made me smile.

I parked my car next to his and got out. The passenger door was unlocked and I slipped inside. "Hi. Miss me?" My voice was breathless, anticipating.

"Took you long enough," he said, fisting his hand in my hair and giving it a gentle tug.

"I'm having a party, Cole. It wasn't easy to get away." I was, in fact, ten minutes early. "But I'm here now."

"Yes, you are."

He leaned across the center console and kissed me. Hard. His mouth tasted of tequila and I sucked his bottom lip between mine, biting it gently. Finally, he released me and I leaned back in the seat.

"You shouldn't drink so much at my house. It's not safe to drive," I said. "It's not safe to be around me, either."

He watched me, his eyes heavy-lidded, but not with sleep. "I can't help it. All I want to do is touch you and I can't. So I drink. It keeps my hands busy."

I laughed. It was a familiar argument. A familiar situation. I kept coming back for more, unwilling to let go of this feeling. "Be careful next time," I admonished. "Brad wasn't too happy to have you pawing at me."

"Yes, ma'am."

I laughed. Cole is hardly the submissive type.

Suddenly, a light caught my eye. Another car had pulled into the empty parking lot. I could make out the figure of a man in the driver's seat, the glow of a cigarette at his mouth. I waited for him to drive past us and he did, parking on the opposite side of the parking lot. He got out, not once looking in our direction, and walked toward the arts and letters building.

"Maybe we should go somewhere else," I said, suddenly nervous. This was where Cole worked; it was too risky even at this hour to be sitting in the parking lot.

"Where are we going to go? I don't have much time."

I hesitated, torn between desire and caution. "Do you know who that was?"

"Yeah. He's in the English department. An okay guy."

I sighed. "Shit."

"Look, he's probably just picking up some paperwork or something," Cole said. "He'll be gone in a minute."

I watched the door, waiting, willing the man to come out, get in his car and drive away. I needed Cole. The door didn't open.

"Kiss me," Cole said.

I obeyed, leaning across the console and taking his face in my hands. We sat like that, separated from the waist down, kissing and touching each other until the windows fogged and I was squirming in my seat.

"You are so beautiful," he said. He stroked my hair, trailing his fingers down the collar of my blouse to the swell of my breasts. "I need you."

I glanced across the parking lot. The car was still there. "Are you sure?"

Cole nodded. "He's probably not going anywhere for a while."

I didn't bother to point out his contradiction. I reached for his belt and undid the buckle, then unfastened his pants. He leaned back, letting me unzip him and pull his erection free of his pants. He was rigid, thick, ready. I whimpered softly as I leaned over him and sucked the head of his cock between my lips. I licked him gently, tasting his arousal; that familiar salty-sweet taste unlike that of any other man I'd ever been with. I dreamed of that taste, looked for it in things I ate and drank, craved it, a thirst I couldn't sate.

He twisted his fingers in my hair, guiding me slowly up and down the length of his cock. I sucked him greedily, hungrily, taking him as far as I could without gagging, then forcing a little more of him into my throat until I did gag and had to come back up. I sucked him the way I knew he liked it, the way Rachel never did, the way it took to make him come.

He dragged me off his cock by my hair, the slight jolt of pain making me whimper with need. "I need to fuck you," he said, his breath ragged.

"I don't have time," I said. "Let me taste you. Please."

He tightened his grip on my hair. "I need to be inside you," he said. "Get out of the car."

He didn't give me time to respond. He was out of the car and opening the passenger door before I could take a deep breath. He reached for me and I let him pull me from the car. I felt exposed, vulnerable, the night air chilly compared to the intimate heat of the car. The other car was still there across the parking lot, a reminder of the risk we took to be together.

"Cole," I protested as he leaned me against his car and unfastened my pants. I stared at the parked car over his shoulder, my pulse throbbing. "We can't. Really. We're going to get caught."

"I don't give a damn," he muttered as he tugged my pants and panties down in one motion. "I need you. Now."

I let him turn me around and bend me over. We were facing away from the parked car now and all I could do was hope the workaholic professor stayed in his office for just a little longer. I braced my hands on the hood of Cole's car, my legs still pinned together by my pants around my ankles. I didn't protest as I felt his fingers between my legs, slipping inside my wet, wet cunt, gliding forward over the ridge of my clit. I didn't complain when he drove his thick cock into me in one hard stroke, burying himself inside me so deep it was almost painful. I didn't tell him to stop, I didn't worry about getting caught, I didn't think about what would happen if the professor chose that moment to leave. I didn't care about anything except the feeling of Cole's cock inside of me.

He held on to my hips as he fucked me, thrusting against me so hard my arms buckled under his weight. I was facedown on his car, the metal cool against my fevered cheek and hard against my hip bones. I cried out as he went deep, my whimpers echoing off the walls of the buildings and bouncing back on me, sounding like the cries of a woman in pain.

I bit my lip to quiet myself, but Cole seemed intent on wringing every sound from me that he could. He wrapped my long hair around his hand and pulled my head back, leaning forward to bite my exposed neck. I whimpered and my cunt clenched around his cock.

"Oh god, fuck me," I moaned. I was beyond caring if someone heard me. I needed Cole to fuck me, fuck me hard and make me forget where we were—and who was waiting for him at home.

I tried to brace myself on the hood, but the slope prevented me from keeping my balance. "Wait," I gasped. I reached back, putting my hand on his hip and pushing him away. He slid out of me and my body felt empty, bereft.

"What?"

I turned around, facing him. "I can't stand up. If we're going to do this, we might as well do it right."

I leaned down to free myself of my pants that were twisted around my ankles. Then I sat on the edge of the car, braced my hands behind me and spread my legs. "Fuck me, Cole," I whispered, offering myself up like a banquet. "Fuck me."

He anchored his hands on my hips as I reached down to guide him inside me. I wanted to stroke my clit with the broad head of his glistening cock, to hold him until he begged to fuck me, but I was too far gone to tease him or myself. I pulled him into me one agonizing inch at a time, then arched my back to take him in deeper, feeling that exquisite twinge of almost pain again. I was oblivious to everything but the feeling of him inside me; then I heard a car door slam.

I tried to push Cole away, even though it was too late for us to save ourselves. "Oh god, Cole, he's watching."

"Let him watch," Cole muttered. "Let him watch me fuck you."

Eyes wide, I stared at the car over his shoulder, barely able to make out the man behind the wheel. All I could see was the glow of his cigarette. He didn't start the car, he didn't leave. He sat there, watching us. Watching me get fucked.

Cole thrust into me hard, over and over, until I didn't care we were being watched. I didn't care about anything except his thick cock inside me, filling me, fucking me. My soft whimpers and moans were the only sounds in the still night air. Cole was silent and stoic as a sentry, fucking me senseless, fucking me into oblivion.

I opened my eyes and looked up at him. His face was just a dark shadow above me, blending into the endless night sky. He was as indistinct as the man watching us, a ghostly stranger fucking me. I blinked, staring at him, willing myself to see his features. Then, instead of seeing him more clearly, I saw the stars. The night sky, devoid of a moon, was filled with stars. I stared up at Cole as he fucked me, his face obscured by darkness and surrounded by twinkling stars that seemed close enough to touch.

"You want it?" I could just make out the movement of his lips. He leaned closer, brushing his mouth against my neck. "You want to suck me? You want him to watch you suck me?"

"After I come," I whispered, fearing he would pull away before I could finish. "After I come."

I wasn't sure he heard me, but his thrusts became more shallow and at just the right angle to stroke my G-spot. I strained forward, pushing my hips at him, propping myself up on my arms to get closer, to pull him deeper. I came in a gush of fluid, my entire body wrapped around him as my cunt tightened and rippled around his thick cock inside me.

"Yes, yes, yes," I screamed, the echo of my voice ringing in my ears. "Fuck me!"

"Now, take it, now," he said, pulling me off the car by my hair and pushing me to my knees.

I opened my mouth wide, wanting to taste him, even while my body still throbbed in orgasm. Cole guided his cock into my mouth, thrusting his hips forward so that it slid across my tongue and hit the back of my throat. I gagged, but instead of pushing him away, I grabbed his hips and pulled him closer, relaxing my throat and swallowing as he started to come.

Cole moaned. Cole, who was always so quiet, moaned loudly as I took his cock deep into my mouth and swallowed everything he could give me. He loosened his grip on my hair, but I didn't move away. I sucked him gently, not caring that my every move was being observed, lingering over him until my knees ached from kneeling on the hard ground. Finally, slowly, I released his cock and he helped me stand.

Cole held me, both of us naked from the waist down, and the incongruity of it made me want to laugh and cry at the same time. The moment was over before I could make sense of my feelings and he was pulling up his pants and handing me mine.

We got dressed silently and quickly, without looking at each other or the car across the parking lot, still there, the driver a witness to our indiscretion.

"Thank you," Cole said, touching my cheek. "I love you."

"I love you, too." My voice was shaky with emotion. "Be careful going home."

When I made no move to get into my car, he hesitated, glancing at the car across the parking lot. "I need to get home before Rachel starts worrying. Are you okay?"

"Fine." I nodded, as if that decisive movement would convince him. "I'm just going to stand here for a minute and catch my breath."

"Okay." He didn't move. "Are you sure you're all right?"

I looked up at the night sky, filled with more stars than I had ever seen in my life. They seemed so close, as if they were falling on top of me. Tears filled my eyes and the stars twinkled. "I'm fine. Just go, Cole."

He went. I didn't watch him leave, I never could. Instead, I watched the silhouette of the professor as he finished his cigarette and then, when the amber glow was extinguished, I got in my car and drove home.

COUPLES WELCOME

Erica Dumas

C OUPLES WELCOME blinks the big pink neon sign outside, but I don't feel very welcome.

The bar is small and smelly and packed with men. Barely clad women my age and younger slink among the patrons giving lap dances, and a pair of dancers are doing a girl-girl scene up on the low stage, their hands roving over each other's mostly naked bodies as they kiss deeply.

The men look at me as I pass them; the dancers look at me with sour expressions, obviously disapproving of the fact that I'm taking eyeballs away from them. If it was up to me, I would turn around and flee. But it's not up to me; that's what I love so much about our relationship. You don't ask me; you don't suggest. You tell. You told me, "We're going to a strip club," and drove out to the Cat Lounge by the airport. I'm dressed for it—short minidress, high heels, no stockings, no bra, just a slip of fabric on my nether regions under the dress. I know my nipples, braless, show through this dress, especially when I can feel them hardening under the gazes of the male patrons. But that's another thing you didn't ask. You told me what to wear. You grip my hand in yours and lead us to a cushioned bench far from the stage.

A topless waitress—nude, in fact, except for a thong and high heels—comes by and takes our drink orders. They only have one kind of drink here—house beer, and it tastes like dishwater. I gulp it anyway, and you lean back on the bench with your arm around me, your pants stretching as you get hard watching the dancers. I don't know whether to be jealous or turned on. Turns out I'm a little of both. A brunette in a garter belt and fishnets goes slinking by, shooting us a flirtatious glance.

"I like her," you tell me. "I think she's the one."

I shiver; the one for what? I'm already wet, not knowing what you plan to do. You make eye contact with the dancer and she heads back toward us.

"Hi there," she says. "Having a good time?"

You clutch me close and smile. I can't bring myself to make eye contact with her.

"A lap dance would make it a lot better," you tell her. "How much?"

"For you or for both of you?" she asks, leaning down and smiling.

"For her," you tell her, and I feel my heart pounding.

She looks at me like a lion sizing up its prey. "Twenty dollars," she tells you. "It's normally thirty, but hell, for her I'll give you a discount."

You hold up two twenties, wink at her. She leans toward you, cocking one hip, and you slip the money into the front of her G-string. "You want to watch?" she asks.

"Of course."

"There's more privacy in the back. Come on."

You practically have to drag me out of the seat. Not that I'd ever dream of saying no to you, but my heart is a jackhammer inside my chest; I feel dizzy and unsure. You lead me, she leads you. She takes us into a darkened corner near the back of the club where there's nobody sitting, where there are no tables. You guide me onto the padded bench. The surface is velvet, soft; you take your place a few feet away in a wooden chair turned toward me.

She stands over me, smiling, her breasts clasped by a tight black bra. Her nipples are visible through the lace.

"Sit on your hands," she says with a smile. I do, and she climbs into my lap as a new song starts. She straddles my thighs, facing me, and reaches back to unclasp her bra. The tiny black lace garment comes forward and reveals her breasts—natural, not fake like most of the girls'. She leans forward and brushes them over my face, bumps the hard nipples against my cheeks.

I feel my own nipples hardening. I see you watching with an expression of deep satisfaction on your face, and my heart pounds faster. She begins to grind in my lap, and I close my eyes and moan softly. She lowers her face and brushes her cheeks against mine. I breathe deeply. I can smell her—perfume and feminine sweat. I realize my legs are slightly parted. You're looking up my skirt. When she neatly rolls over and sits in my lap, the weight of her small body works my thighs open. I can feel the pressure of her tailbone against my clit. She leans all the way back, her shoulder blades touching my nipples, her long black hair all silken and fragrant around my face and against my shoulders, her lips close to my ear.

"You don't really have to sit on your hands," she tells me. "That's just something we have to tell you. But that's why we do it over here in the dark."

When I hesitate, she perches herself on my lap and reaches down to take my wrists. She guides them up to her belly, then her breasts, and the feel of her nipples so hard against my sweaty palms is electric. I hear myself moaning softly. She writhes on top of me, rubbing her hair over my face, grinding her ass into my lap.

She's quite the acrobat. She arches her back and pushes her face against my neck. Then she kisses me, her tongue trailing over the soft underside of my throat. I shiver. She presses my hands more firmly around her breasts.

"I like it when girls come in," she whispers into my ear. "You're so much more fun to dance for."

I can feel the silk of her smooth-shaved thighs rubbing against mine as she squirms and arches in my lap. Her hands on mine encourage me to stroke her nipples, and I can feel the energy coursing from her body to mine. I lean back into the soft bench and realize I'm relaxing. I'm relaxing and getting turned on. When she smoothly lifts herself up and rolls over again, coming down straddling my legs, I get more turned on. I see her pretty face coming in for a kiss, and my lips, parted, open wider for her. Her tongue tangles with mine and she neatly begins to unbutton the front of my dress.

"You don't mind, do you?" she whispers when our lips part.

By then, I'm beyond minding. I'm not attracted to women, or I thought I wasn't. But the feel of her against me is making my blood pound, the pleasure race through me. When she's got the front of my dress open she reaches in and gently eases out my breasts, giggling a little. "I hate bras too," she says. "So uncomfortable." Her tits brush against mine, the nipples so hard as they send tingles of sensation through my body. She kisses me again, grinding on top of me. It doesn't even occur to me that other patrons might be watching. I don't even really care.

The only thing, in that moment, is the feel of the stripper's body against me and the heat of your eyes on us. I spread my legs a little further and I know you can see well up my skirt, which has snugged its way up my thighs. When I see you over the stripper's shoulder, you're smoking a cigarette, feigning disinterest. But your eyes are anything but disinterested.

She reverses herself again, sitting in my lap and leaning back, her slender fingers caressing my face. She cocks her leg up and draws one high heel up the inside of my lower thigh. She leans back and kisses the side of my face. And then the song is over.

She wriggles herself out of my lap and leans down to retrieve her bra.

"Did you like it?"

I just stare at her with my eyes wide, moaning softly.

She crosses in front of me, bends down next to you and whispers something in your ear. Then she nuzzles the side of your face slightly, and disappears into the swirling, smoky darkness.

You crush your cigarette out on the floor as I quickly button the front of my dress, blushing. You take my hand and guide me to my feet. Then, one arm around me, you lead me back into the hall that leads to the restrooms.

There's a fire exit there, but somehow it's not alarmed. You push your way through it and we're in an alley, so dark, so black that I can't even see you at first. But I can feel you—taking my wrists, one in each hand, and pushing me up to the hood of an old, rusted-out car parked right under the NO PARKING sign.

By the time my eyes have adjusted you've got me bent over it, right at the front wheel well. I look down the alley, desperately, an exhibitionist thrill mingling with fear of discovery, but there isn't a chance I could say no. You get my skirt pulled up and my panties tugged down to my thighs. They fall to my ankles and I step out of them as you nudge my legs open with your knees.

I hear your buckle rattling as you undo your belt and unzip your pants. You slide one finger up my slit, just to test me, and I moan as it touches my clit. I'm wet. I'm incredibly wet. I'm ready to have you. I'm ready to be *taken*.

You've had me like this before—quickly, urgently, without preliminaries, me bent over and being taken from behind. You've had me over the kitchen table, over the kitchen counter, over the back of the sofa and the side of it, over the four-poster bed in a B&B, over the tailgate of your truck in our suburban garage. But you've never had me like this—over an illegally parked car, in the wrong part of town, out by the airport, in the alley behind a strip club.

You enter me in one swift thrust, with my body tensing and my back arching as your cock takes me savagely, tenderly. I feel it pushing all the way in, my cunt easily accommodating you because it's so incredibly wet and I'm so incredibly turned on. Pleasure runs through my body as you begin to fuck me. I've missed a button on the front of my dress, and it's come open even before you reach under and pull at it. The hood of the car is still warm from being driven. It feels smooth against my hard nipples. You drive into me with deep thrusts, as I stretch my arms out over the hood of the car and hold on. My hair scatters across my face and now I can't see anything even if it wasn't dark. There are no streetlights in the alley, which is why you've chosen it. You can have me as long as you want, however you want. Your weight holds me against the car as you surge into me, again and again, almost lifting me off my feet with each thrust. I lose myself in the sensations, in the warmth of the car, in the coldness against my sides and on my back—everywhere you're not up against me. I feel your cock head hitting just the right spot—bringing me close. I'm too afraid people might be watching. I'm too afraid. I couldn't possibly come.

But I do, forgetting myself and moaning, softly at first and then more loudly, finally crying out at the top of my lungs as my orgasm rips through me. You reach around and press the heel of your hand into my mouth, unable to silence me but at least muffling my cries, while you fuck me harder. I come through the whole last part of it, a long, languid orgasm that won't seem to end. My body shudders with pleasure. Your thrusts grow quicker, more demanding—and then your sigh tells me you're filling me, letting yourself go deep inside me. Your last few thrusts are gentler, softer as my orgasm dwindles, as you spend yourself inside me. When you pull out, I can feel the wetness there, the excitement that tells me your come is inside me. I sigh and lie there, drunk with the bliss of it, high with the risk of it. You pull my skirt back down and guide me back to my feet, turn me around with my ass against the warm car hood. You button up the front of my dress, and this time you don't miss a button.

I watch as you kick my panties into the trash in the corner of the alley. You take my hand and lead me down the alley toward the strip club parking lot. I follow you, moist and leaking, unsteady with the pleasure of it. The alley closes in, dark behind us, and when we get to the car you kiss me against the passenger-side door, soft at first and then deeper, your tongue taking me under the big pink neon sign.

You work the remote and the soft *ker-chunk* tells me I can open the door. The pink neon blinks overhead as I ease into the passenger seat. COUPLES WELCOME.

You kiss me once, tenderly, and start the engine.

BUSTED

Sophie Mouette

After the movie, Elle and I parked at the edge of the beach. It was too dark to see much except a hint of paler darkness where the surf hit the sand, but we cracked the windows so we could hear the crash of the waves and the murmur of the wind without getting too cold.

I don't think we intended for things to go as far as they did. I certainly hadn't planned on it, but when her warm tongue entered my mouth and her warm hand crept beneath my shirt and found my lace-encased nipple, all rational thought fled, except for a momentary flash of pleased surprise.

It seemed extra-naughty to be fooling around in a semipublic place with my girlfriend the cop.

Making out in a car is never easy, but when you're young and in lust and have been dating only three months, you make do and don't care about pretzeled limbs. You pretty much don't complain unless something cramps and you have to shake it out or scream.

I wasn't complaining. The briny air mingled with the tea tree scent of Elle's shampoo as she kissed me, leaning across the console to where I sat in the driver's seat. She had this ability to point her tongue and flick strongly, and when she did that against mine, I felt it all the way to my clit—where, sooner or later tonight, I'd feel her tongue for real.

She scraped her fingernails across my nipple and it rose to hard, aching attention. I moaned against her talented mouth and, encouraged, she used her nails to pinch.

Some of my friends laughed when granola-dyke me started dating a police officer, saying it was an obvious case of opposites attracting. But we really do have more in common than base physical urges. I like Elle's taste in old movies and her ability to create a gourmet meal out of my poor excuse of a pantry; she confessed she was intrigued by my obsessions for Swedish heraldry and Italian greyhounds.

So let 'em laugh. At least I was getting some.

And I wanted more. Needed more. I climbed over into her seat to straddle her, whacking my knee against the gearshift and almost elbowing her in the eye in the process. The bruises (for me, at least) didn't matter. It seemed like her hands were everywhere, encouraging me: first on my breasts, then running up and down my back; high on my thighs, tangled in my hair.

I was getting so wet, so hot. I managed to insinuate one of my legs between hers, which meant that one of hers was between mine, and I ground against it as best I could in the confines. I'm a tiny thing, but she's tall and lanky and mostly leg—which helped.

She pulled my shirt over my head and tossed it somewhere, then rained a line of tiny nips along my collarbone as I gasped from the sudden sensations. She roughly pulled the bra cups down so she had direct access to my breasts. I moaned as she suckled one, kneaded the other.

Her cardigan separated as I pulled on it, and at least one button popped, disappearing between the seats to be lost forever. Oops. Beneath it, she was braless, which was no doubt why all the men had been staring at her tonight. Her luscious breasts were pale in the darkness, and although I couldn't get my mouth down on them, I did my best with my hands to return the favors she was giving me.

I'm not really clear on how we got me out of my jeans. My thong, Elle just pushed aside. It was mostly useless by now anyway; I could smell myself in the steamy confines of the car.

"My little firebomb," Elle whispered as her fingers sought my wetness. "You are just insatiable."

I couldn't form a coherent answer. She buried two fingers in my folds, pressed them up into me. I clamped down on them, desperate for release. The combination of thrusting fingers and the thumb she had pressed against my clit and her mouth clamped on my aching nipple was overwhelming. So many sensations, driving me further to the edge.

I crashed over into orgasm, grinding myself against her hand. I clutched the headrest with one hand and pounded against the car's ceiling with the other. "Fuck, yes!"

And that's when a bright light shone in the window and a strident male voice said, "All right, kids, let's break it up in there."

It was the voice rather than the light that caught my attention, largely because my bare ass was facing the window, giving the officer a fine view. I pulled my bra up, and tumbled sideways into the driver's seat, my feet still tangled in my jeans. The action revealed Elle's breasts in all their glory. She yanked the edges of the cardigan together, but not before the cop outside got a nice eyeful.

Shit. *Cop.*

I'd been caught making out in a car before. Even caught by a cop. But never *with* a cop herself. Never when one of my partner's coworkers, essentially, was watching.

Crap.

I reached behind my seat and flailed around for my shirt.

"Jesus, MacIntyre." Elle's voice sounded annoyed rather than embarrassed. She rolled down the window a little farther and glared up at him. "Don't you have anything better to do?"

"Tudor, is that really you?"

"Yes, it's me," she said, trying to button her sweater in the dark. (Lucky her. Even with the missing button. *My* shirt had apparently been sucked into a black hole.) "I thought you had the night off."

"Nah, I'm trying to get in as much overtime as I can before the baby comes." He chuckled. "Lucky me. Wait 'til I tell—"

"You're not going to tell anyone, MacIntyre. The word will get back to Debbie that you saw me naked, and she's got pregnant-woman hormones right now...."

His face fell. "Damn, you're right. Oh well." As he turned to go, he added a "Hey, Destiny," in my direction.

In silence, as if we were both holding our breaths, we listened to his car door slam and the motor rev to life.

"Elle, I'm so sorry..."

To my amazement, she busted out laughing.

"It's all right," she said when she could finally talk over the wild whoops and guffaws. "Did you see his face?"

"You mean as he was ogling my tits? You owe me a new shirt, by the way." (She didn't, really, but I figured I'd keep my options open. Never turn down the opportunity for new clothes.)

"Destiny, it was priceless! Poor guy couldn't figure out where to look. He was really embarrassed."

"*He* was embarrassed? It's not like his ass was on display for the world to see."

She laughed again. "I don't know about that. It's one thing to be ogling seminaked strangers; it's another to realize you were ogling your coworker and her girlfriend."

I gave up on the search for my shirt (a bra doesn't show any more than a bikini top, right?) and started the car. Before we got very far, Elle was laughing again.

"You should have seen his face, Des. His eyes were like dinner plates. I think he'd been watching awhile before he turned on the flashlight…and then saw the one person on the force who can consistently best him at target practice."

This time I managed to laugh as well. I hadn't been so embarrassed since I was in junior high school and Julia Ruiz discovered I had pictures of actresses in my locker instead of boy-band members, but it was pretty damn funny. And as I was laughing, something dawned on me.

The way I was squirming wasn't just from embarrassment. Some little part of me was turned on, not so much by what actually happened as by images running through my head.

I wasn't quite sure how to broach the subject, but the more I thought about it, the more I wanted to say something. I finally choked out, "Too bad it was MacIntyre."

"If someone had to catch us, he's perfect. He's a good guy, and he's so scared of doing anything to upset Debbie right now that he'll keep it quiet."

"Yeah, but he's still a guy. A man catching us is just embarrassing. A woman catching us and watching for a while—that might have been hot." My voice kind of trailed off at the last bit.

Elle made a funny choking noise. "What?"

"I said it might have been hot." I looked away, focusing

completely on the road, not quite able to meet her eyes after that admission.

"Hm. Sounds like somebody's a bit of an exhibitionist...."

I couldn't tell from the tone of her voice whether that was a good thing or not. We hadn't been together long enough for sharing our wilder fantasies to come easily. Had I found a limit?

I figured the answer out pretty quickly, though, when I felt her hand brush my nipple.

"So, my darling Destiny likes the idea of a stranger watching her getting off?" she said, still chuckling a bit, but in a throaty, sexy way now. I arched my back, pushing my breast toward her palm.

"I guess so. Bit of a surprise for me, too," I admitted.

"Really?" She captured my nipple between two strong fingers and I temporarily lost the ability to speak. Not so much from arousal—although all my blood seemed to have diverted from my brain to my nipple and from there to my clit—as from shock. Elle was not the sort to grope me while I was driving. In a parked car, sure, but not while the car was actually moving. She'd seen too many gruesome car accidents to distract the driver—and I was certainly distracted. I gripped the wheel a little tighter, because much as I wanted to return the favor with interest, I was afraid of what might happen if I let my attention, or my hands, wander.

"I like it too," she went on. "I like the idea that someone saw me making you scream. I like the idea that someone else got to see how goddamn beautiful you are when I'm driving you crazy." She twisted the nipple. "That makes me hot."

I was writhing in my seat, amazed that attention to my nipple was doing as much as it was. Sure, my nipples are sensitive, but not normally to the point of me soaking my jeans with juice because of a little tweaking. Especially not right after I'd just come.

It was a good thing my house wasn't too much further. Between arousal and giggle-fits over MacIntyre's expression, I was rapidly becoming a road hazard.

Usually when we end up at my place, we take Lorenzo and Lucrezia, my spoiled little greyhounds, for a walk. That night we barely had the patience to let them run around the fenced-in yard and do their business. As they zipped around the yard, Elle and I were stripping each other's clothes off, enjoying the naughtiness of getting naked outside. Not that anyone could really see over the privacy fence unless they were on the neighbor's roof—it was the principle of the thing.

What if they were on the roof? What if they were watching? The fantasy added to the excitement.

Elle all but threw me onto the bed. "You are a far naughtier girl than I knew, Destiny," she said.

"How do you feel about being fucked by a really naughty girl?" I reached into the back of the toy drawer, groped a bit, and pulled out the big red strap-on with the dragon-shaped head. We'd still been having so much fun with hands and tongues that we hadn't played with the toy collection much yet, but tonight seemed like the perfect time for Mr. Fiery to come out.

Elle blinked as if mildly confused as she watched me adjust the belt around my hips. Then a slow grin lit her face. "That thing rocks! Thank you, Venus!" she exclaimed. "You sent me the woman of my dreams!" She pulled me close to her into a long, deep kiss.

Such a long, deep kiss; such a sultry kiss, that it almost changed our plan, because it led to more kissing, and from there to nibbling, and from nibbling to stroking—the kind of progression that made old-fashioned parochial schoolteachers say that

French kissing causes pregnancy. Not that it would do *that* in our case, but anyway...I got so distracted I almost forgot the strap-on was even there.

Elle subtly reminded me by rolling me over onto my back and sinking onto the toy.

"Oh yeah," she moaned. "Why didn't you use this on me before?"

"Seems like you're using it on yourself," I said. "Not that I'm complaining. What a great view." And it *was* a great view; her long, lean body crouched over me, rocking back and forth.

"No better than MacIntyre got of you," she said through clenched teeth.

"How much do you think he really saw?"

"Who knows? I just like..." Her voice broke off and she began to grind her hips against me, getting my clit involved in the action from the pressure. I grabbed her hips, moved her in the way I knew I'd want to be moved in her position. Not coincidentally, it was good for me as well and for a little while any attempt at talking was impossible. We weren't quite at the screaming point yet, but we were certainly getting close.

After she caught her breath a little, Elle picked up the sentence where she'd been forced to leave off. "I like the idea of someone watching. Or maybe more the idea of you getting off on being watched. Because you do get off on it, don't you?"

She reached down between our bodies so she was touching both our clits. At the same time she did something with her hips that obviously was very, very good for her.

She arched backward, her hand still stroking both our clits. I could see her ab muscles quivering.

"You get off on that idea, Destiny—and I get off on how much you like it." I swore I could feel her contractions, although that didn't make a lot of sense through a silicon dick.

And then everything collided—the stimulation from earlier; the idea that MacIntyre was riding out on his lonely patrol with a big hard-on, thinking about us; Elle's hand caressing me; Elle's beautiful body riding me; the scent and heat and slickness of her; her excitement.

Stars, I thought before all thought became impossible. *You really can see stars when it's this good.*

Friday night, I got a phone call from a desolate-sounding Elle. "I know we had plans tonight, sweetie," she said, "but we're shorthanded today and I drew the short straw to cover the late shift."

Safe behind a closed door in my office, I cursed volubly. We didn't just have plans for the night. We had positively evil, depraved plans.

"I'm bummed too," she said, "but I do have an idea that'll get us through until I can get to your place." Her voice dropped to a whisper. "Around ten o'clock, go into the bedroom and start playing with yourself. I'll be thinking of you then, picturing what you're doing to yourself and getting all hot. Will you do that for me?"

My pussy clenched. "You bet!"

"And then I'll be off shift around two and wake you up in the nicest possible way."

She hung up, leaving me blushing and somewhat damp.

Wow. Elle and I were still very much on a classic New Relationship High, but for the last couple of days the sexual tension had been running even higher and this pushed it further yet. I flashed back to the incident in the car. The embarrassment had faded by now, burned away by amusement that our encounter with MacIntyre had ended up sparking so much lust.

I could hardly wait until ten o'clock to get started. Okay, let's be honest. I didn't exactly wait—nothing wrong with a bit of warm-up, right? I decided to save my actual orgasm for when I knew Elle would be thinking about me, but I curled up with a collection of erotica and teased myself over and over. By ten, I was aquiver, more than ready to explode and send all kinds of lust through the ether to Elle.

I opened the curtains in the darkened bedroom to get a view of the moon peeking up over the privacy fence, cracked the window for some air and settled down in the comfy chair facing the window. The bed might have been a more logical choice, but I felt closer to Elle looking out into the night where she was. Besides, no one could see in the window without opening the locked gate and entering the backyard—but given the fantasies Elle and I had been swapping lately, I could admit I liked imagining that someone might. I spread my legs, closed my eyes and began to diddle.

I'd grabbed my favorite dildo out of the toy drawer just in case, but decided to start with just fingers and imagination. I pictured Elle, stuck two fingers into my dripping pussy, imagined they were her fingers finding my G-spot, imagined her voice whispering hot, filthy things in my ear.

I was so primed that I felt myself starting to quiver almost instantly with those little shivers and contractions that lead up to the final explosion. So close, so hot...

And then a harsh light penetrated my eyelids. I jumped, opened my eyes to the flare of a big Mag-Lite. What the fuck? I scrambled, attempted to cover myself. Burglar?

"Police! Freeze," exclaimed a familiar voice. "Or better yet, heat it up."

I couldn't see her clearly with my dazzled eyes, but the laugh that rippled through the window, low and sultry, recharged me instantly.

"You liked being caught by cops? Well, sweetheart, you've been busted this time! Don't stop on my account."

The flashlight went out. I heard the sound of zippers, fabric rustling.

I clicked on the lamp next to me to give her a better view.

We hesitated. I don't know what was going through her head, but I know I was torn between heat and desperate self-consciousness. Should I pretend I didn't know she was there? Or that she didn't know I knew?

When my blood has rushed between my legs, my brain does *not* function well.

Then Elle whispered, "I'm watching you, Des." She sounded like a dirty old man in a peep-show booth, and I felt a thrill shoot through me.

"I'm looking at your gorgeous little breasts and your pussy, which is all swollen and wet and just the prettiest pussy I've ever seen, and I'm watching it twitch because it knows it's being stared at and it likes the attention."

I heard a noise, and guessed that she was stroking her clit. Getting off by watching me. Oh, Christ, this was good. This was really, really good.

"Make yourself come for me, babe," she murmured. "Just like you came on my hand the other day with MacIntyre watching. Because you know what? I couldn't get a really good look at you then and I just hate the idea that he might have had a better view than I did."

The combination of her voice and the mental picture of her fingers making a lazy circle on her wet button mesmerized me. With one hand I opened my labia. With the other, I slid the dildo into my very slick opening.

"So now I get to watch," she said. "Remember that, babe: A cop is watching you play with yourself. You've been busted.

"Just like MacIntyre busted us. But I'm watching you now. I get to see your perfect breasts, and that intent look you get on your face when you're about to scream. You're going to come for me any second now, aren't you?"

I heard the change in her voice. My eyes had adjusted enough that I could see her face, dimly, through the window. I saw her flushed face, the look of urgent concentration, the slightly crinkled brow. She was close herself.

I could also see my own reflection in the glass: spread-legged, a fat dildo stuffed inside me.

"Do it," I begged. "Come with me."

It's a funny thing. Your face screws up when you're coming and you roll your eyes and make uncouth noises and if you've seen yourself at that moment you probably think you look ridiculous. Still, there is absolutely no vision as glorious as the face of someone you're crazy about when she's in the throes of orgasm. When Elle began to shudder and her face transformed like that, right before she began to cry out, I started coming too, and it was the sight of her face, not my hands or the dildo or the original fantasy that sparked us, that pushed me to ecstasy.

Eventually—after a romp in the backyard and another in the shower—we settled down to fall asleep in each other's arms. Just as we were drifting off, Elle began chuckling.

"What is it?" I mumbled. It was hard to be grumpy after coming approximately forty-seven times over the course of the night, but I'd almost been asleep.

"I didn't tell you whose partner I was covering for tonight." She'd already explained that she'd only been scheduled to work until nine-thirty. She had, in fact, engineered the whole thing to act on our new fantasies.

"Oh my god!" I said. "You got stuck with MacIntyre!"

"Talk about the longest evening in history." She moaned

dramatically, the back of her hand against her forehead. "Every so often I'd catch him looking at me, and he'd see that I saw, and he'd go all red again. To make it worse, we had to patrol the beach parking lot."

I laughed. "So, did you catch anyone in the act?"

She pulled me closer. "Only you, Destiny. Only you."

X-RAY SPECS

Heather Peltier

I was never into comic books as a kid, but my brother Steve worshipped the things. I mean, over the years he read them all—from old reprints of *Detective Comics* to the comic-book version of the Twisted Sister story. He tried to get me to appreciate the finer points of graphic novels and the subtly Greek tragedies of *Batman* and *Spider-Man,* but I wasn't listening. I had the same experience with Jordan, whom I dated for three years, and who turned our shared apartment into an archive for his treasured *Sandman*s, *Preacher*s, and *Love and Rockets.* No matter how many times he would chortle and exhort the virtues of comic books, I never bothered to read them. They just never grabbed me. Even a friend who did his master's thesis on the homoerotic imagery in superhero comics couldn't talk me into liking them. I could appreciate Superman's well-sculpted torso, sure, but I was always more of a sucker for skinny geek boys.

Enter Joel, the skinny geek boy, and his girlfriend Kerry, the buxom bad girl. I guess it took sex, wine and '50s kitsch to make me really appreciate comic books.

Divisadero Comix is a mélange of pop culture, with a stunning collection of tie-in lunch boxes—from *Superman* to *Star Trek: The Motion Picture*—lining its walls above impressive bins of ancient, dusty comic books, and the shelf over the counter covered with a neat array of He-Man dolls, Micronauts, and G.I. Joes. Joel and Kerry, the couple who own the place and are its only employees, are both obsessed with the stuff. Well, I guess it's mostly Joel, but Kerry can certainly appreciate a good Flaming Torch thermos or Fonzie belt buckle.

It really is quite impressive. There are potato guns ordered from the back of *Fantastic Four* comics long before Joel, Kerry or I were born. There are little metal robots from the '50s—worth a thousand bucks apiece, Joel once told me—displayed under glass in the back of the store, and the window displays change weekly, drawing in a stream of tourists and comic-book nuts. Joel and Kerry figure if they keep the place interesting enough, they can stay in business.

I guess it works, sort of. I mean, I did live upstairs from the place, but I never would have come down and bought all those comics if I hadn't spotted the window display that featured Jabba the Hutt eating Barbie.

Then again, it wasn't really Jabba the Hutt that kept me coming back. It was the fact that Joel and Kerry were the cutest couple I had ever seen in my life. I guess they were about what you'd expect—both twentysomethings with tattoos and piercings, Joel with his long blond hair streaked with purple and Kerry with hers dyed raven black, Joel wearing mostly skintight shirts that showed off his slim physique and always—no matter what day of the week it was—wearing tight leather pants. And Kerry's outfits were equally exciting, little plaid schoolgirl skirts and knee-high boots showing off fantastic legs sheathed with fishnets or spiderweb stockings.

And her tops. I mean, Kerry is cute, don't get me wrong. But I sometimes have trouble looking her in the eye when I'm talking to her. I'm a slim girl, and I guess I've always been attracted to busty ones. If Joel, with his dark eyes, haunted smiles and skintight pants hadn't kept me coming back for more, then Kerry, with her low-cut shirts and full lips, would have.

But it's weird flirting with couples. You never know when or whether to make the move. For us, it finally boiled down to a pair of X-ray Specs.

It was late on a summer Saturday; I'd spent the day in the park on my bicycle and after locking it in the lobby of my building, I'd stopped in at the comic shop for a visit before going up to my apartment. Exercising always makes me feel really aware of my body, and I was still wearing my workout clothes—tight sports bra, cycling shorts and tennis shoes. I was way too sweaty and exhausted to feel sexy, but something made me feel invigorated, too. I made a halfhearted loop through the stacks of comics, not really wanting to pick up anything new—I still hadn't read the last pile Joel had talked me into. Kerry and I chatted as she counted out the register, and Joel fiddled around with a display of '50s tchotchkes. They both looked particularly cute that evening, despite the long day they'd just put in.

I wandered over to Joel and smiled at him.

"What are those?" I asked, pointing to a pair of plastic glasses with weird-looking spirals on the lenses. "Three-D glasses?"

Joel made an insulted sound. "My dear Sarah, these little gems of the midtwentieth century are"—he put them on with a flourish—"X-ray Specs."

"X-ray Specs?"

"You used to be able to buy them in the back of comic books," said Joel, looking me up and down with a devilish smile on his face. "Still can, sometimes."

"What do they do?" I asked.

He took a long, slow moment to lean over the counter, close to me, and look me up and down slowly once, then twice, then a third time.

He grinned at me. "They let you see through people's clothes," he said.

"Nuh-uh," I said, grabbing for them.

He stepped back from the counter, out of my grasp. "Yes-huh," he said, still staring at me. "And if you don't mind my saying so, Sarah, that's a very naughty tattoo."

I instinctively felt my skin prickling. I stood up straight and tried to think of what to say. I giggled.

"You lie," I said. "I don't have any tattoos."

"Oh yes you do," said Joel, looking right at my crotch, where I sport one of my two tattoos. I felt my blood run cold, then hot in a weird rush of sensation. "And it's a naughty one."

The tattoo just above my pubic bone is a small, full-color one of a '40s-style blonde bombshell—touching herself. I felt suddenly exposed, half of me believing that Joel really could see right through my tight bicycling shorts, could see the tattoo—could see my pussy. I knew it was bullshit, but I felt suddenly naked, strangely excited at the thought of Joel undressing me with his eyes. With that, I could feel my nipples hardening, and I became painfully aware that they were quite evident through the sports bra. Joel's red-spiraled eyes lingered over them shamelessly. He licked his lips and smiled.

"You are so full of shit," I said. "You lie, you lie, you lie," I laughed. "You can't see through my clothes."

"Kerry," said Joel. "Get over here."

Kerry came over, and Joel slipped off the glasses and handed them to his girlfriend.

She put them on and gasped.

"Sarah, really! A blonde bombshell masturbating? You *are* more naughty than you let on. And you really should wear underwear with those shorts."

It was silly, really. I knew they were joking with me, but for a moment I actually believed they were both looking at me, inspecting my naked body. I felt my nipples harden still more and felt a warm pulse go through my pussy. I had been flirting with Joel and Kerry for months, but I never really thought anything would happen—I mean, I didn't even know if Kerry was bi.

"You guys are so full of it."

"Then how did I know what your tattoo is?" smirked Kerry. "And you really aren't wearing any underwear."

"Cut the crap," I giggled, turning and walking away from the counter. Kerry handed the X-ray Specs back to Joel; he donned them and followed me with his eyes.

"Great ass, too," he said. "That one's cute, too. Who's 'Jordan?' "

The hairs on the back of my neck prickled, and I swallowed nervously. I was starting to really believe it—really believe they could see through my clothes.

My other tattoo, you see, is my ex-boyfriend's name on a red heart—bright red, on my ass. I got it only three months before Jordan and I broke up, but I decided to keep it—it kept things interesting whenever I got naked with people.

I don't know what I thought. I guess part of me believed they could really see through my clothes.

I turned around. "Give me those," I said, half smiling.

"No way," said Joel. "You think I want you evaluating my genital piercings?"

"Tit for tat," I said, coming toward the counter, leaning over and reaching for the glasses.

Joel, who's six-four and skinny, swept the glasses off his face and put them on the top shelf with the line of Skeletor figures.

"Gimme!" I said bitterly.

Kerry sighed and came around the counter. "I've got a much more interesting way for you to evaluate his genital piercings," she whispered, leaning close to me.

I froze, my eyes narrowing.

"Yeah, I bet you do," I said, smiling.

"We're almost done here," said Kerry. "Why don't you come upstairs for a drink, Sarah?"

I hesitated, not sure what to say.

Kerry put her arms around me and kissed me, softly, on the lips.

"I mean, we've already see you naked," she laughed.

I could feel my face flushing hot as she took me by the hand and led me back to the little door that led to their upstairs apartment.

Joel was right behind us. I glanced back and saw him pluck the glasses off their shelf and put them on, smiling and shaking his head as he looked at my ass. I suppressed a giggle, feeling his hot gaze on my body.

As we mounted the stairs, I could hardly believe I was doing this—I mean, they were adorable, hot, and sexy, but I had never really thought anything would happen with them. And now here I was, after a long workout in the park, sweaty and still dressed in workout clothes, going up to have a drink with this couple that had just embarrassed the hell out of me.

Problem was, it had really turned me on.

I guess I'm a little bit of an exhibitionist. Just the idea of these two sexy flirts looking me over naked, discussing my body so casually, had excited me. The fact of the matter is, if they'd just up and asked me, I might have been too nervous to say yes. But after working me up like that, they had me at their mercy.

Kerry and Joel live in a single converted room above their comic-book store. They've decorated it in the esteemed style of a late-eighteen-hundreds New Orleans bordello, complete with opium pipes hanging on the walls. The memorabilia was relegated to the shop; their apartment had more dignified and decadent adornments. The place smelled of incense, alcohol and the close scent of their bodies. Just smelling it excited me.

The only furniture in the small room was a low-slung velvet loveseat and a beanbag chair. I wondered where they slept.

I guessed I would probably get to find out.

"Red wine okay?" asked Joel as Kerry steered me toward the loveseat. "Or would you prefer scotch?"

"Definitely scotch," I said, sinking into the soft velvet as Kerry and I leaned close on the sofa. She began toying gently with my short hair and then kissed me on the lips, this time opening her mouth slightly. My lips parted, too, and I felt the warmth of her tongue against mine. I put my arms around her and felt her body pressing hot against mine. My pulse quickened as her hands moved down my back, then around to my belly. She pulled up my sports bra and her mouth descended to my hard nipple, suckling it. I moaned and ran my fingers through her raven-black hair, feeling a surge of pleasure go from my nipples to my pussy. She caressed one breast with her hand while her tongue traced a path around my nipple and she bit down gently.

"Since we already know what you look like naked," said Kerry, "you may as well take those clothes off...."

My heart was beating so fast I couldn't have said no even if I'd wanted to. Kerry slipped my sports bra over my head while

I kicked off my shoes, and then she peeled the sweaty spandex shorts off my lower body and ran her hands up my thigh as I sank naked into the velvet of the sofa, feeling it caress my body.

"It's smaller than it looked through the glasses," said Joel, squeezing onto the sofa next to me.

He handed me my scotch, neat, and I took a quick drink before kissing him, tasting the red wine he'd sipped. His tongue was pierced. As we started to make out, Kerry's mouth returned to my breasts and she kissed them all over, her hand wriggling its way between my thighs. Lost, naked between these two clothed lovers, I let her part my legs and felt her fingers caressing my pussy. I was incredibly wet.

"I really quite prefer you naked," said Joel between deep kisses. "Especially these marvelous tits of yours."

"Tit for tat," I said.

I helped Joel and Kerry out of their clothes and the three of us twined together on the sofa. Kerry was as beautiful out of her clothes as she was in them. She had tattoos all over her body— an intricate green ivy with flowers around her round hips, a dagger above her pussy, a Chinese character on her upper thigh. Joel was long and lean, and muscled, as I'd suspected he would be—but I didn't expect the long, smooth curve of his cock to be so beautiful, so inviting. They took turns, one kissing me while the other teased my breasts, kissed down my belly. Then came the moment when Kerry kissed further down, spread my thighs, and melded her mouth to my pussy.

I moaned. I reached out for Joel's cock, grasping it, and leaned down so I could take it in my mouth.

Kerry's skilled tongue worked its way between my slick lips, teasing my clit and making me want Joel's cock even more. I swallowed it all, long and slim as it was, and I felt Kerry focusing on the rhythms of my body as my hips pumped up against her face. She rode me flawlessly, seeming to sense exactly what I needed to come and then pushing me further. By the time I began to shudder as my climax approached quickly, my mouth had slipped off of Joel's cock and I was gripping it with my hand, my lips parted wide in a moan of orgasm.

The two of them wrapped their arms around me, Kerry kissing me on the lips and letting me taste my own pussy. When I went back to sucking Joel's cock, she joined me and we traded off, kissing between strokes up and down on its hard length. Joel moaned louder, his hips rising, his ass lifting off the sofa.

"All yours," whispered Kerry, kissing me. "If you want it."

I did. I closed my mouth around Joel's cock and slid up and down, hungry for him. When his cock jerked and I felt the first stream in my mouth, I decided in that instant to swallow it all. I missed only a tiny drop as he pumped into me, and Kerry bent forward to lick that off of my chin.

Joel was still moaning as Kerry and I kissed deeply. I could taste my juices mingled with Joel's come.

I spotted the glasses on the coffee table. I reached out and snatched them before either one of them could stop me—but this time, they didn't try.

I put them on.

Both of them were a big fuzzy mess of weird lines and radiant images.

"Hey!" I said. "You can't see through people's clothes with this." I laughed.

"It's because we're naked," said Joel, his voice thick with postorgasmic pleasure.

"Bullshit," I said, waving my hand in front of the glasses and watching the vague shadows dance back and forth incomprehensibly. "Tell me the truth. How did you know about the tattoos?"

Joel shot Kerry a look.

"Well," said Kerry. "I guess it might have something to do with the fact that Jordan buys his comics here."

"That bastard."

"His lips get real loose about ex-girlfriends' tattoos when you throw in a few free books," said Kerry, her face reddening.

She smiled at me weakly. "Are you mad?"

I picked up my scotch from the coffee table and lifted it to my face, inhaling its aroma, loving the way it mingled with the scent of sex.

"At Jordan, maybe," I said, eyeing Kerry's illuminated, skeletonized face. "At you two...no."

I smiled and kissed her, feeling vaguely nauseous as the room swirled, distorted, around me.

"Good," said Joel. "Because I put sea monkeys in your scotch."

"Keep it up," I said. "There's a potato gun with your name on it, buster."

"Such a filthy mouth."

I drank the scotch.

FORCEFUL PERSONALITIES

Dominic Santi

From the moment I first saw Christa, I wanted her naked and kneeling at my feet.

Looking was easy. Getting her to submit took some serious negotiation. She was wearing a power suit and doing her level best to fleece my start-up company into providing a cut-rate contract for the corporation she represented. My cock twitched at the sight of her shoulder-length blonde hair brushing against hand-tailored silk that complemented the almost startling blue of her eyes. Her breasts were full, firm mounds. She had the most perfect ass I'd ever seen.

It wasn't long before the innuendo in our conversations showed we both knew we were discussing a private as well as a public deal. Sparks flew between us with every offer and counteroffer. Christa made it clear she was only interested in doing things my way if it got her what she wanted. And she was willing to play dirty. She had a habit of chewing her lower lip that kept me so hard I would have been embarrassed if I were the type to blush at an erection.

I wasn't. Apparently, neither was Christa. She couldn't keep her eyes off my crotch. Each time I caught her looking, she just closed her jacket over the aroused points of her nipples and sucked on that full, red, pouty lip. Then she smiled and went back to business.

Two days later, I was so horny I swung the negotiations to an agreement that gave her more than I'd planned, though it still turned a tidy profit for me. The initial gut punch of meeting her had progressed beyond a simple hunger. I wanted her willing, and I wanted her for good. The day we signed the contract, I ratcheted our private negotiations to the next step by convincing my new colleague to join me for a celebratory dinner.

Christa told me I didn't need to pick her up—or open doors or choose the restaurant where we were going. I told her I did, keeping my hand firmly on the small of her back as I guided her into Alberto's, where I'd requested a secluded, candlelit table in the back. She was dressed for sin in a short, backless, skintight black knit sheath that showed off the delectable curve of her ass. No obvious panty lines. No garter bulges where the seamed black silk stockings rose from her four-inch strappy heels and disappeared under a hem that was barely a hand span below her crotch. The dress was cut low enough in front to show the cleavage between firm, high breasts I had no doubt would fit perfectly in my hands. She wasn't wearing a bra. However, when I looked closely, and I did, blatantly, I saw the almost imperceptible line at her waist telling me she was wearing a very tiny thong.

"You're gorgeous," I said as the waiter showed us to our table. When I moved my hand against her back, her nipples hardened. My hand slid lower, rubbing the string of the thong. I was done with innuendo. "You're overdressed."

"Thank...I beg your pardon?" She turned so fast she tipped on her heels. I steadied her and pulled out her chair for her.

"You heard me."

The look on her face was priceless as she slid into the chair. Ignoring the waiter, I leaned forward and spoke softly in her ear. "The dress is perfect. Take off the panties."

I moved past her to take my seat and turned my attention to the waiter. Christa's eyes flashed as I told him to bring me the wine list and two glasses of ice water. As soon as the waiter was out of earshot, Christa tapped her fingernails on the tablecloth and gave me a look that had brought Fortune 500 CEOs to their knees.

"What makes you think I'm taking my clothes off for you?"

I wasn't going to be the one kneeling. I handed her a napkin. "I'm going to be your lover, eventually your husband. The sooner you're naked, the sooner I'll give you orgasms."

I didn't expect Christa to let that pass unanswered either. But from my position, I could see the waiter returning with the water pitcher. As she drew in her breath, the waiter reached her side and picked up her glass. She snapped her mouth closed, biting her lip and drumming her fingers on the table as he filled our glasses. I covered her hand with mine, stroking my middle finger in her palm while I rubbed my thumb over the back of her knuckles and ordered my favorite wine. Eventually, her hand relaxed and she smiled tightly.

"You have quite the little fantasy world going there." She pulled her hand back as the waiter again left us. "Do you suffer such delusions often?"

I caught her fingertips and lifted her hand to my lips. "I believe in making fantasies come true." I kissed her fingers. When she shivered, I sucked the tip of her index finger into my mouth.

Her eyes softened as a beautiful blush crept up her cheeks. I bit lightly, then sucked again, smiling as she once more set her teeth to her beautiful, full lower lip.

"I'll stop anytime you want, anytime you ask me to. All you have to do is say 'no' or 'stop' or 'don't.' " I ran my teeth over the full pad of her finger. "Trust me, Christa. I'm going to make you beg me to take you, and I'm going to make you come so hard you scream."

"This is ridiculous," she muttered, blowing her bangs off her forehead. But she didn't move her finger from my lips. Each time my teeth touched her skin, she shivered.

"It's sexy." I kissed her fingertip and set her hand back on the table.

The dining room was filling, but the light was low and tables nearest us were still empty. I took an ice cube from my water, trailing it over the exposed upper curves of her breasts.

"What on earth?" She grabbed my fingers, her eyes flicking quickly around the room to see if anyone had seen us.

I shook my head. "We want each other, Christa. What others think doesn't signify."

For a moment, she chewed her lip. Then she smiled and dropped her hand back to the table. The melting ice was running down over her skin and between her breasts. Her nipples were pebbled like rocks, the wet fabric clinging like a second skin as she shivered again. When the ice was almost gone, I dropped it into her cleavage. This time, when she touched her tongue to her lip, she licked slowly and sensuously.

"I don't know why I'm letting you do this," she whispered as the waiter appeared again. I left my hand against her breast.

"You're letting me pleasure you because it feels good, and because I'm going to make you come like you never have before. Don't move." Although the waiter didn't bat an eye,

Christa flushed and looked away. I ordered for both of us, looking only at her as I carefully eased the top of her dress lower. I tucked in the edges of the damp fabric until her nipples were barely covered. When the waiter left us again, I picked up another ice cube.

"Tell me you want me, Christa."

The waiter was seating another couple at the table in back of Christa. With my hand innocently against the edge of her dress, I slipped the ice inside, so it rested on the top of her nipple beneath the clinging fabric. Christa gasped. The man being seated turned toward us. I ignored him, keeping my eyes on her more wildly flushing face as the wet circle grew over her breast. When the man turned away again, I picked up another piece of ice. I held it in my hand over her other breast.

"I dislike waiting, Christa."

I wanted her so badly I would have waited forever, but I wasn't going to tell her that. Instead, I watched the pink tip of her tongue flick in and out as she worried her lip. My cock was so hard I had no doubt the front of my pants was as wet as the front of her dress. Her skin was warm beneath my motionless fingers. She shivered as the water from the melting ice dripped onto her. When the waiter walked past with the drinks for the other table, she took a deep breath and whispered, "I want you."

I slipped the rest of the ice cube onto her nipple. She shook as I smoothed the folded top of her dress back into place.

"The sooner you obey me, the sooner you'll receive your pleasure. Remember that."

Christa nodded as I stroked the back of my fingers down her cleavage where the water had run. Her skin was cool to my touch. I knew my hand felt warm.

"Go to the restroom. Take off your panties and throw them away. Keep the top of your dress just as I have it."

Christa hesitated only a moment. Then she nodded and got carefully to her feet. She didn't bother looking at the rest of the room. The beautiful, strong-willed woman I wanted so badly I hurt just smiled, turned, and walked slowly and seductively toward the hall. With each step, her hips swayed with a practiced gait that let me know she had made her decision.

By the time she returned, the ice had melted, leaving her dress clinging to her pointed nipples. When she was seated, I rested my hand where her stocking met the bottom of her dress, and I rewarded her with a slow, wet kiss.

"I'm proud of you, Christa." The tablecloths at Alberto's were long enough to hide a multitude of sins. I slid my hand over the top of her stocking, then over the even silkier skin at the top of her thigh. Then higher.

"Was it difficult to obey me?"

The neatly-trimmed thatch was slick with her juices. She shuddered as my fingers slid into her slit. With a soft moan, she slid forward on the seat.

"It was harder than hell." Her eyes closed as she sucked her lip between her teeth. "It was worth it."

I laughed softly, my fingers pushing deep into her cunt as my thumb settled on the protruding nub of her clit. I rubbed in slow, firm circles. When she gasped, I curled my fingers toward her belly button and rocked my hand.

"Come for me." My voice was harsh, but I couldn't help it. I nearly came in my pants watching her.

Fortunately, the first quaking shudder was almost immediate. The other tables were filling, and the waiter was approaching with our food. Christa was still trembling when I pulled us both up. I smiled indulgently at her bemused look as the waiter served us and quickly left. Christa gasped as I once more quietly slipped ice cubes over her nipples. Then I picked up my wineglass and proposed a toast to all our forthcoming mergers. Christa clinked her glass to mine, and with her eyes still smoldering, dug into her dinner.

I was tempted to insist on having dessert, for the pure pleasure of watching her face as I licked chocolate mousse off her fingers. But now that Christa had decided what she wanted, the naked desire on her face had me so hard I could wait no longer to get her alone in the car.

The waiter was too well trained to comment when I asked for a cup of ice to go. I tipped him handsomely. Then I slid my arm around Christa's shoulders and guided her out through a room now full of people who were much too busy to notice the passing of any two individuals.

It took Christa a minute to finesse her heels and that short skirt back into my car, though she was much less concerned about letting me look up her skirt than she had been on the way to the restaurant. When we were finally in, I opened the small container of ice. I took out two pieces, wetting them briefly in my mouth. Christa gasped as I slipped them in the now familiar positions on her nipples. When I picked up a third cube, she raised an eyebrow at me. I grinned and closed my palm around it, until water dripped out the side of my hand.

"Slide down in the seat and spread your legs."

She hesitated for only the briefest second. There wasn't much room, but the sight of her hiked-up skirt and the tops of her stockings framing her naked, well-trimmed pussy, was something I would take to my grave.

"I can't believe I'm doing this!" Her laugh was shaky as she slid down against the butter-soft leather. "I love it. Ooh!" Her eyes closed as I slid the ice down and up her slit, then back to circle the hypersensitive nub.

I put her hand on the ice, then directed her fingers to

continue stroking in the same, slow, lazy pattern. With my left hand, I started the car. The familiar high pitch vibrated through me. "Keep circling."

Aside from the impeccable food and superb staff, one of the pluses of Alberto's was that it was less than ten minutes from my home. I pulled the car into the driveway and pressed the button to close the security gate behind me. I parked under a secluded tree on the far end of the circle and cut the engine. My cock throbbed at the glimpses of Christa's pussy as she swung her legs out. I grabbed some condoms and lube from the glove compartment. Then I took her elbow and steered her to the gazebo at the side of the house. I dumped the packets on the bench and sat down hard beside them.

"Straddle me." I pulled Christa roughly over my legs and onto my lap. Balanced on her high, teetering heels, she was just the right height. I yanked the front of her dress open and sucked a cold, turgid nipple into my mouth. She muffled a scream in her hand.

"Don't." I pulled her hand from her face. "I want to hear you come." Then I turned my head and sucked in the other nipple. It wasn't long before her moans became sobs and her hands were fisted in my hair, holding my head to her as she ground her naked pussy against my pants.

When her groans were almost constant, I urged her up enough for me to open my fly, shove down my pants, and free my cock. I grabbed a condom and a couple of lube packets. Then I pulled up her dress and guided my cock to her pussy lips. Her cries were desperate as she gripped my shoulders.

I lifted my lips from her nipple long enough to growl, "Fuck me!"

She instantly obeyed, inching her feet forward for balance. I sucked her nipple back into my mouth. I kept sucking, alternating from one nipple to the other while I guided her hips with one hand and diddled her cool, slippery clit with the other. Orgasms rolled over her in waves as her cries grew louder and louder.

I wanted more. I wanted all of her. And I wanted her to crave it. As the next waves rolled through her, I kneaded her bottom, squeezing and caressing until she finally pushed back against my hands. Then, I slowly pulled her cheeks apart.

"Turn around. I'm going to fuck your ass."

For just a moment, Christa stilled. Then she took a deep, shaking breath and looked me right in the eye.

"I've only done that once before. It hurt."

I twitched my cock inside her. "Do you believe I'll hurt you?"

Again, the slightest hesitation. Then she shook her head. She rose up and carefully moved her legs over me until she was straddling me facing the other way. Bracing her hands on her knees, she slowly sat back, lowering herself until she was positioned over me. I emptied an entire packet of lube over my latex-covered cock. Christa jumped when I smeared the slippery gel over her anus. She jumped again, gasping, when I pressed one well-slicked finger inside, then another. She moaned in pleasure when I slowly moved them in and out.

"That feels good," she whispered, shivering as the fingers diddling her anus stretched her sphincter open. With my other hand, I held myself firmly against her.

"My cock will feel better."

She gasped as the slippery tip started in. I put both hands on her hips and eased her to me. "Slowly, Christa. Finger your clit. That's it. Keep your fingers moving, no matter what."

Her bottom was cool from the meltwater that had run down between her cheeks and she was relaxed from her climaxes. As her weight settled onto me, my cock head slid slowly through. She gasped so loudly it was almost a cry. For a second, her whole body trembled. Then she moaned, long and slowly, as I pulled her down and my cock slid in to the hilt.

"OOH!"

The hot, tight spasms milking my shaft were sending me over the edge. Her fingers moved frantically between her legs as I set my hands on her waist and slowly fucked her ass up and down over my cock. Christa's cries were desperate now, pleading with me to fuck her ass hard and fast, begging me to make her come. Her shudders were almost continuous as her quivering ass sucked the orgasm through my cock.

I thrust up hard, shouting her name. She screamed and ground against me, her pussy juice squirting as she teetered on her shoes and I spurted load after load of hot, creamy spunk up her quaking ass.

I fell back into the seat, holding her tightly. Christa collapsed against me, her head resting on my shoulder as she shook and panted. When her breathing finally turned to nervous giggles, I smiled.

"Holy fucking hell!" She laughed, snuggling back into my arms. She sighed as my softening cock slid slowly free. She glanced down at the dress bunched at her waist. "I can't believe I just did that—and I'm still wearing my damn dress!"

"You told me you weren't taking your clothes off for me," I said.

"That was silly of me," she laughed softly. "You have my permission to take my dress off me, anytime you want." She turned and kissed the side of my face. "Sir."

I grabbed the front of her dress and tore it from her in one sharp rip. Christa giggled and snuggled deeper.

I kissed her shoulder softly. "We'll keep a small dressing room with your clothes for work and outside social occasions. But otherwise, when you're home, you're going to be naked, submissive, and supremely well fucked."

Christa sighed, but she didn't move to get up. "I suppose this means your bossiness is here to stay?"

I laughed and swatted her bottom. "It always has been."

She put her teeth to her lower lip. The gears were wheeling again. "What about my heels and my stockings and my jewelry?"

My cock jumped. I bit the back of her neck. "You can keep those."

This time her chuckle was low and contented. "Deal." She picked up the remnants of her dress and walked naked toward the house, her hips swaying seductively in the moonlight. "It's good to be home."

All I could do was laugh. My Christa had definitely been worth the wait.

THE POET, DYING

Simon Sheppard

When people looked at Antony Considine, they saw an elder statesman of American letters, or a poor old man on his last legs, or a doddering fool. Some people saw all three. Yes, putting words on paper was, the poet had come to realize, quite an odd little way to piss away one's life.

> *Embarkation, forever ruined*
> *yet perfect,*
> *or sometimes this is all you get,*
> *this ache*
> *of noplace and everywhere*
> *all at helter-skelter*
> *once.*

Considine had hired the two boys—"hustlers," in common parlance—to come over in late afternoon. As he'd rationalized it to himself: *Might as well. My cancer will handily outrun the dwindling of my bank account.*

And now here they were, big as life, in Considine's ever-bohemian apartment.

The lads hadn't come as a matched set, but were hired from two separate ads in the back of the local gay newspaper. The first boy, Dillon, was one of those perfect young men whose very existence both amazed Considine and broke his heart. Dirty blond hair, beautiful face, startlingly smooth skin, a tightly knit body beneath his clothes, nipples temptingly visible through his thin shirt. Considine knew—as he'd always known—that he would never, could never, write a poem as lovely as Dillon. Or whatever his name really was.

The other was, intentionally, something else again. The aging poet had trawled the ads, done a lot of research before settling on Kev. That's not to say that Considine found Kev unattractive. On the contrary, the boy seemed enormously sexy—attainable, and therefore hot in ways that the flawless Dillon wasn't. Kev was, in fact, the sort of sex partner Considine had, more often than not, himself ended up with. Back when he was a kid, an unbeautiful youth, in the closeted 1950s, he had gone to demimonde taverns to ogle the Dillons of the world—in fact, the pretty hustler suddenly seemed oddly familiar—but it was usually the Kev du jour who would end up sucking his cock.

Kevin, then. The English had a word for it: *podgy.* Somewhat overweight, ungainly. An open, unremarkable all-American face that would no doubt mature into surpassing ordinariness. And while Dillon's skin was glowingly flawless, Kev's was...less so.

Nonetheless, Considine found Kev absolutely charming. Not literally fuckable, of course; Antony Considine was in no shape

to fuck *anyone* anymore. Often, he barely could rouse himself
to wank.

> *The tremors of possibility:*
> *the clichés of butterfly, spring, a car crash.*
> *The one I choose to call "you."*

But he'd been saving up for this. Not just money—in fact, he
was far from penniless, though his honors had outrun his earn-
ing power. No, he'd been saving up energy, storing little parcels
of lust, to be unloaded when Kev and Dillon arrived. And now
here they were, the three of them in Considine's jumbled living room, with its musty, marvelous smell of aging books. And
Kev's rather awful cologne. Considine wished he'd remembered
to tell the boy not to wear any, or at least to make a more pleas-
ing choice. Ah, well.

"Take your shirt off, Kev."

"Me too?"

"No, just Kevin, for now."

Considine settled back to watch. The pain pill was just beginning to hit, and he felt, for one thrilling-but-surely-fleeting
moment, that the whole world was *billowing*.

Kev was surprisingly good at his job. Rather than just blun-
dering into seminakedness—or even worse, doing a kitschy
striptease—the podgy boy slowly unbuttoned his denim shirt,
staring directly into Considine's eyes. One button after another,
but the poet could barely tear his gaze away from the boy's plain
face. Kev's naked torso was fleshy and nearly hairless, except
for one small patch of fur between his generous tits. His nipples
were fairly wonderful: large, perfectly pink, and symmetrical.
And his convex belly looked supremely strokable.

Everyone, everybody,
paroxysms of violet, this particular
day
which, like us, will broach no end.
But solid.

"Now, um, Dillon, go over to Kev and undo his pants. That's
right." Considine was aware of what used to be called "a stirring in his loins." He had been leaning forward, somewhat
tentatively, on his well-used sofa. Now he sat back to watch the
show. Kev had kicked off his shoes, and Dillon was on his knees,
helping the other boy step out of his pants. Kev was wearing
simple white Y-front briefs, not even designer ones, just Fruit of
the Loom. He was, indeed, the Hustler Next Door. And, from
the look of things, exceptionally well-endowed.

Dillon's pretty face was just inches from Kev's crotch, but
neither of them moved a muscle; they just stood there for a long
moment like the first scene in some pornographic *tableau vivant.* Then Dillon looked in his direction, quizzically, as if to say
"What now?" And Considine realized he hadn't really sketched
out what he intended, whether he was going to be director, or
just set the scene and let it play itself out.

For now, some guidance seemed necessary. "Go on, pull
down his underwear. But leave his socks on." *As though,* he
thought, *we were all in some delightfully dirty video.*

Kev's newly revealed dick was, indeed, as prodigious as
promised: long and thick, nicely tapered, glossy head half-
revealed by foreskin. My god! Life—what was left of it—was
sweet.

Without prompting, Dillon nuzzled his face against Kev's
cock, two beauties. The poverty of words: The dying poet realized that nothing he could put on paper could ever match the

moment's breathless...well, *glory* wasn't too strong a word, even it were rarely applied to two on-the-job hustlers putting on a show. Yes, *glory* it was.

> *Solid as a single-winged butterfly*
> *that nobody sees, like death: the Buddha's*
> *practical koan-joke.*

Dillon, without prompting, had grabbed the base of Kev's cock and was licking the tip. Considine reached down and started rubbing his crotch through his baggy old-man's pants.

"Does that feel good, Kev?"

"Yes, sir." *Sir.* What a well-brought-up young man! Unless he meant the "sir" as a mere intensifier, as in "Yes, sir, that's my baby."

They were *both* Considine's babies. For now. As long as the cash held out.

"And what would feel better, Kev? Anything you can think of?"

"My whole dick. In his mouth."

"You heard, him, Dillon." At that, the pretty boy expertly slid his full lips all the way down to Kev's copious bush. It was, obviously, quite a piece of meat to deep-throat, and Considine admired the boy's skill. He had a not-very-great viewing angle, though.

"Here, swivel yourselves around so I can better see the cock sliding in and out. And get closer. Please." Just because he was paying, that was no reason not to be polite.

They moved in, Dillon scooting on his knees. Now the blow job was only about a foot and a half away from Considine's failing eyes.

And I would like to make it clear
to you...
Damn, I forgot.
Something, maybe, about butterflies?
Jesus...

He had bought the sight of these two boys, this sucking-off, but it was nonetheless exciting. In reality—and he had to admit it, however guiltily—the very fact that this apparent lust was purchased, that it was, at base, just a for-cash construct, was exciting to him in and of itself. But then, he'd always thought too much; that was, he'd often consoled himself (no matter how inaccurately), a major reason he'd never in his long life managed to hold on to a boyfriend for long.

"Okay, Dillon. Spit out the dick and stand up." His former college students, all full of respect for his putative genius, would no doubt be shocked to hear him speak that way. Fuck it.

Young Dillon was on his feet now. Yes, yes, he reminded Considine of someone, somebody from a long time ago. What was his name? Gone.

"Clothes off."

Unlike Kev's artless artistry, Dillon's disrobing was utterly nonlyrical, a mere shedding of clothes in order to expose The Good Stuff. *But then*, Considine mused, *I suppose when Nature has so graced you, you can just slack off on the details.*

Dillon's cock was smaller than Kev's and, disappointingly, only half-hard. But Considine, whatever else he might have been, was no size queen, and at least the kid hadn't shaved his bush, the way so many of those porn-boys he'd seen on the Internet did.

Maybe it was about us. Or maybe moths
or something. These rivers,
this eternal day...

"Hands above your head."

Considine was crazy about the sight of underarm hair, always had been. Dillon's, he saw, was unfortunately on the light side. Considine hoped at least he wasn't wearing deodorant.

"Now turn around, Dillon. That's it. Now bend over."

He was beginning to thoroughly enjoy this, this show he was arranging on the fly. And speaking of fly... Oh god, should a poet of his renown be thinking of bad puns?

"Spread your cheeks."

A perfect hole, pink and as fuckable as the rest of him. And it was surrounded by whorls of dark-blond hair, a sight that Considine always enjoyed; more than once, he'd mused that ass-hair was shamefully underappreciated. But then, he'd always been drawn to buttholes; the porn websites that held his interest featured ass as well as dick. He was especially fond of close-ups of Eastern European boys' holes, nail-bitten fingers spreading cheeks apart, revealing—if he was in luck—sacramental pink membrane.

"Kev, there's a rubber on the table over there. Put it on."

"Does he have to?" Dillon asked, still upside down. "Condoms irritate me."

For a moment, Considine, rather taken by surprise, hesitated. No, he wouldn't be party to anything dangerous. He knew about illness, entirely too much. Dillon, apparently, did not. At least, not yet. "Yes, he does."

Kev, with a bit of difficulty, unrolled the latex over his bulky cock. Aside from everything else, rubbers—even those as thin and transparent as the one the poet had provided—made dicks look so damn unattractive. Considine sighed. Homos, true, no longer had to hide, but some things had changed for the worse.

"How you want us?" Kev asked.

"Dillon on all fours." *Like the pretty little bitch he is.* "You fuck him from behind."

Antony Considine's penis was fully hard now, a little miracle, even if the miracle had been pharmaceutically facilitated. At his age, you took what you could get. He opened his trousers and fished out his erection.

Beautiful Dillon got down on his hands and knees, Kev kneeling behind him. A slight hitch: if they were positioned so Considine could watch the penetration, Dillon's incredible face wouldn't be fully visible. So at their client's direction, the boys fetched a mirror from the bedroom and propped it up in a corner of the cluttered room. Kev's cock had remained gratifyingly erect throughout. Dillon was soft now, apparently unexcited by the thought of husky Kev and his hefty dick.

Now Considine, stroking himself, could see it all. Dillon's tightly knit body gleaming slightly with sweat. Kev lubing up his cock and sliding it, with some difficulty, up Dillon's ass. Kev grabbing Dillon's hips, careful to let Considine witness the details of the fucking, and pounding into the increasingly sweat-soaked Dillon. Too bad the sense of smell declined with age; Considine could only imagine the full impact of the heady blend of body odor and ass. Kev's somewhat pendulous belly and tits trembled, and his face took on what Considine chose to take as an expression of bliss. When the strokes went especially deep, the otherwise impassive surface of Dillon's handsomeness was broken by rippling winces. Seeing that—perfection undone by the putative Act of Love—made Considine very happy. Very happy indeed. *If I could,* he thought, *I would see him destroyed.* Followed by *Oh, you melodramatic old queen!* And, dick in hand, Considine smiled, smiled again. He looked down at himself. His cock was, he thought, even after all these years, in its own way quite magnificent.

Magnificent.

As though nothing, not all the anthologies, the academic honors, could measure up to simple flesh.

"You boys..." Considine began. He could not, though, think of what to say next.

Suddenly, unbidden, unruly Kev scrunched up his face and thrust all the way into Dillon. Coming. Dillon's lovely hustler-boy face looked surprisingly nonplused. And Considine...Considine himself, somewhat startlingly, felt his body—a body that had lately seemed nothing but his enemy—overpowered by spasms of lust. No! He wasn't ready. Not yet. Not yet. Not...

> *...this*
> *moth-eaten,*
> *eternal day.*
> *You.*

Perhaps in pleasure, perhaps something else, the great poet closed his eyes.

COMMAND PERFORMANCE

Teresa Noelle Roberts

Kneeling in the dim, sticky space, Michelle fingered her collar. Her nervous sweat beaded clammily on her skin. She didn't know what strings her master had pulled, what dubious connections he had called upon, to place her in a peep show, waiting to exhibit herself for strangers.

Someday she might find out, but she hadn't asked. All that really mattered was that Master wanted her to display herself in this way, safe from strangers' touches, but at the mercy of their eyes.

(Master. Always Master. His name was Jonathan, but she couldn't remember the last time she had used it to his face. And what Master called her, more often than not, was Girl or Little One or Sweet Thing or simply Slave. He hadn't taken away her name, but the possibility remained out there on the horizon, terrifying and tantalizing.)

She'd only seen one peep show before. Master had brought her, held her against him as the woman in the booth strutted and mugged and showed her lithe, leggy body for them. She'd ended up kneeling before them, her knees open, then slowly leaning back until her body was on the floor, leaving them a view of her cunt. Her breasts, which had seemed suspiciously large and firm, hadn't moved as she lay back, proving they were fake. Master put in another quarter to keep the girl exposed like that and opened his fly, pushing Michelle to her knees on a floor soiled with strangers' spunk to suck him off.

If the girl in the booth had noticed, she hadn't reacted. She'd seemed rather bored with the whole thing, her only real spark showing in the first few seconds when she made eye contact with Michelle. The woman had smiled then, recognizing another slut, another draftee into the army of depravity.

But this slut-in-a-booth was not bored, not at all. Frightened and aroused in equal parts, Michelle couldn't be sure exactly why she was trembling: fear of a stranger's impersonal desire or need to experience it for her master's gratification. Her pussy was slick and the smell of her heat was starting to hide the ancient funkiness of the space, but her mind had other ideas. She remembered her master's hands on her body the night before, more gentle than usual until she'd tried to balk at this game, saying she wasn't an exhibitionist. Then he'd closed his hands around her throat, not to choke, but to remind her of his power, his strength, and whispered, "You will do this because I want you to."

The hands on her throat weren't what convinced her. She knew he wouldn't tighten them, wouldn't harm her. It was his eyes, gone an intense ice blue in that moment, boring into her and making her admit that she did want to do it. Not because she wanted to show her body to strangers—that was something she dreaded, exposing her imperfect body with its wide hips, its too-small breasts, its too-round belly—but because she wanted to please this man. Because she could not say no to anything he demanded of her. Always she had had some doubt what she would do if he wanted her to do something she found terrifying, something she truly wished to resist.

Now she knew. She might fight it for a bit, but ultimately she would take a deep breath and say, "Yes, Master."

And then she would get wet enough that you could sail a cruise ship into her cunt and berth it.

It didn't matter that she was queasy from nerves, that every centimeter of cellulite in her body felt magnified, that she wasn't sure she could move at all from the relative comfort of kneeling, let alone go through the simple routine that she and her master had worked out. She was want personified—not want for this particular act, which still frightened her if she let herself think too much about it—but for her master, and for the pleasure she knew he'd take in this. She might not be an exhibitionist, but he was definitely a voyeur. An exhibitionist as well, in his own way: he didn't like to show himself off, but rather to show her off, show off the result of all his training and effort. And knowing how much he enjoyed it made her fear worthwhile.

In the fleeting quiet that remained to her, she pictured him: blue eyes that could be cold and stern, but never hard, and as often as not radiated impish humor; broad shoulders; solid legs; a height that towered over her. A man who was both gentle and dangerous. A man who had ordered her to strut her stuff before strangers.

She clung to the mental image of him. She knew he was out there, in one of the booths, but that she was to focus on the other customers, the ones not intimate with her body and her heart, the ones whose gaze was not a familiar comfort.

The ones who had not had OWNED tattooed on their asses in kanji.

The music blared, startling her. Def Leppard, she thought,

but she wasn't sure. Not the sort of music she usually listened to, but she let it take her, its pumping rhythm, its sheer brazen volume. The first window opened and she crawled toward it.

Crawling she had down to an art, a catlike slink that made her feel both sensual and subservient. She made eye contact as she had been directed, then licked her lips and forced herself to smile at the two guys in the booth.

She didn't know what she'd expected the customers to look like—the proverbial dirty old men, she supposed. These were boys, maybe eighteen, wearing hoodies emblazoned with the logo of a nearby college, and for a second her confidence flagged. Wouldn't they be disappointed to look at a less-than-slim woman in her thirties when the world was full of pretty, slender girls their own age?

The answer came to her in her master's voice: *They didn't come here to see a pretty girl. They came here to see a slut, a depraved little slut exhibiting herself. Someone just like you.*

They didn't want pretty. They wanted hot. And one thing Master had taught was that she could be hot.

Michelle rose to her knees, then rocked back onto her heels, flashed her legs open too quickly to be anything but a tease. Back down onto the floor, she rolled and stretched, then stood up in a way that gave a good shot of ass, and turned to make eye contact with the next window that had opened.

Master.

She missed a beat. He smiled, winked and made a shooing gesture, telling her to keep going. She winked back, turned to give him a shot of kanji-emblazoned ass and strutted forward, cupping her breasts like an offering for the youngsters in the other booth.

Their window began to close, but they pumped more quarters in.

Another window opened. She angled herself, stuck her butt out at that window and looked over her shoulder to leer at the new customer, this one the stereotypical old guy in a shabby raincoat.

Michelle stood, turned, repeated the pose looking back at the boys, and then, daring greatly, toward her master.

Heat bored through her. *I'm doing this for him. For that man, right there. Because he told me to. Because he owns me. Because he likes showing me off. Because I love him.* She swore she could smell him, leather and cinnamon soap, over the pervasive, shabby odor of the peep show, even over her own rising musk. She wondered if he could detect the flush of her arousal, see the glint of moisture on her thighs. She wondered if the others could. At the thought she felt herself getting more wet.

Maybe she was a little bit of an exhibitionist after all, under Master's direction.

She glanced down dubiously at the dirty floor, remembering the blatant, nasty way that Master had ordered her to end the performance.

They weren't here to see Michelle. They weren't here to see the pretty, refined woman she could be under other circumstances. They were here to see a slut. To see Master's slut.

Deep breath. She was going to do this—for her master, who had made her into this slut, turned on by displaying herself on his orders.

She sat down on the floor, then spread her legs wide, showing her dripping pussy to the audience. She ran two fingers down her slit, then raised them and made a V for Victory sign, showing to each window in turn the glistening strands of moisture between them.

The old man had his fly open, his cock hanging out. The boys weren't so bold, but she could see from their eyes they wanted to do the same. She glanced toward her master, but he was smiling calmly behind the façade of control he never lost until he chose to.

With one hand, Michelle opened her pussy lips, exposing the wet, gaping hole to hungry eyes. She had never felt so open before, so vulnerable. On the one hand, she wanted to close her legs, slink away, hide herself in shame. On the other hand, her body ached. Master was what she needed, Master's cock, Master's whip, anything he would be willing to use to get her off.

What she had was Master's order to get herself off in a very specific way.

And although she couldn't have imagined doing such a thing before others on her own whim, it was his order, and because it was his order, she suspected she'd be able to come from it. That was the real thrill for her, not one particular act or another, but knowing that, even if she were touching herself, she was doing so under his command.

One by one, she put her fingers into her mouth, sucking and licking lasciviously, making a great show of it, maintaining eye contact first with the boys, then with the old man, who was beating off magnificently. Once her fingers were slicked, she held them up for the onlookers to see, then plunged all four at once into her pussy.

Just as Master had ordered.

"But what if I can't get them in all at once, Master?" she'd asked. "Can I do it one at a time?"

He'd chuckled, said, "Oh, you'll be able to, my little slut. I know you," and pushed four of his much larger fingers into her.

Then, she'd come almost instantly, aroused beyond reason already by his terrifying yet exciting plan.

This time, she wasn't allowed to, not yet, but that gave her time to really feel how stretched she was, how full. Tight, but not painfully tight. She was able to move them in and out gently as she stroked her clit with her other hand. Lovely.

She'd been mentally prepared to put on a good show, complete with porn-worthy over-the-top writhing and moaning, in case she couldn't actually bring herself to orgasm. It didn't seem like her acting skills, such as they were, would be needed.

She looked at her master and her cunt began to flutter, contracting hard and fast against her invading fingers. He raised his thumb, in part a thumbs-up gesture, in part a reminder that she wasn't done yet.

She worked in the thumb as well. She couldn't fist herself, but all five fingers were in her cunt and she knew that to the men so avidly watching it looked as though she might. They were waiting for it, hoping for it. The old guy was grimacing, his hand moving blurringly fast on his dick. One of the young guys was stroking himself through his jeans. As she met his eyes she licked her lips, and saw him unzip in response, pull out a stiff young cock.

She looked again to her master, saw him mouth the word, "Come."

Flicked her clit one last time and obeyed him.

As always.

As she did, she lost herself in his eyes. Crying out, writhing, impaled on her own hand, Michelle came for her master in complete privacy, not noticing as strangers' spunk splashed on the peep show floor in tribute to her command performance.

THE KEY

Sage Vivant

Of all the tourists who invade Santorini each summer, Americans are my favorite. They don't bother to learn much Greek before they get here, but they are friendly enough to make you forgive them.

My brother and I have run our restaurant, the Octopus, for nearly twenty years. Our sign is not in English but still the Americans come. Christos and I prefer the Greek customers, but in the end, everybody's money is the same.

Only half the restaurant is enclosed. It faces the narrow walkway through Oia. The east side is completely open and overlooks the clear, sparkling Mediterranean. Tourists usually gravitate to that side. Locals come inside so they can talk with me and my brother, hear the music, be close to the bar.

So, I was a little surprised when this gorgeous American woman sauntered in and sat at the bar. We do not have one of those fancy bars like you'd find in an upscale restaurant or hotel.

There are only five tall chairs and they aren't even comfortable! Greeks sit, drink, and talk for hours so, generally, they settle in at tables rather than the bar. It's more relaxing. But she came in, just as the dinner crowd was starting up, sometime around eight o'clock or so.

Her dress was the brilliant blue found in the Greek flag. We paint homes and buildings with that color, too. It represents valor, the sky, and the peaceful water.

I knew she had to be American because the dress hugged her body like any man's hands would have. Americans are famous for their blatant clothing, leaving so little to the imagination. But in this case, I did not object to the lack of subtlety. Beautiful full breasts and a nice, round ass for balance. Greeks love shapely women and believe me, this one was a feast of flesh.

I greeted her because I greet everyone who comes to the Octopus. She had an easy, pretty smile but she had that dismissive air women put on to discourage small talk. For me, not talking was just fine. I could stare at her luscious tits more easily if I didn't have to pretend to watch her face while we spoke.

Everyone noticed her. Women shot wary, judgmental glances at her while the men stole furtive, hungry ones when their wives weren't watching. She ordered a glass of the house wine when I told her it came from my winery.

She spoke to no one and pretended to be very interested in her napkin. A beautiful woman, alone, who speaks to no one—what is such a thing? I wondered. This woman intrigued me. She exuded warmth and sensuality but held on to it tightly, as if she might otherwise lose it. I decided she was probably meeting someone, so I shifted my attention back to running my restaurant.

No one spoke to her, probably for nearly half an hour. I gave her another glass of wine, my treat, to be kind but also to see if a little alcohol might loosen her up. The longer I watched her breasts rise and fall in that blue dress, the clearer the image became of my hands full of them. I offered her some *mezethes* but she refused. Without food, the alcohol would act faster and I was anxious to see that happen.

A tall man with a goatee came in, dressed nicely, also definitely American. He approached the bar and I thought, "Ah, here is the man she has been waiting for." Their eyes met but no words passed between them. The man sat at the bar, leaving an empty chair between them. He ordered my vineyard's wine, too.

He was only human, so his eyes kept roaming over her body. I confess I walked by her more often than I had to, just to appreciate the curve of her behind warming the seat of my very lucky chair. She ignored us both.

And then I walked by as she crossed her legs and pointed her toe at the man. She shifted in her seat to do this. Her eyes stared at her glass, but her foot was only a few centimeters from his leg.

My English isn't great but I heard him ask her if he could buy her a drink. She looked at him, finally, but refused the drink.

She didn't look away. Instead, she stared at him with such bold curiosity, I felt like an intruder in my own restaurant. His color deepened as she let her eyes travel from his face down to his crotch.

He spread his legs once her gaze settled on his lap. They were facing each other now.

"This is how people meet in America?" Christos muttered from behind me. His words made me realize I'd been staring, so I forced myself to visit a few tables. It was still too early for the locals, so I had to make conversation with a few Germans. If you've met any German tourists, you know this is no easy task.

Christos caught my eye as I was telling some of them how to catch the bus to Thira. He raised his eyebrows in the direction of the bar. I looked over to see the voluptuous beauty with her wineglass in one hand while she traced her cleavage with the other. Her foot now slid up and down the man's shin. I could see his bulge from across the restaurant.

The man had that look on his face that every man, regardless of nationality, knows too well. It is the face that betrays desire, the look that says, "I await the tiniest sign of invitation." It is, sadly, the way we look when all we want is to fuck the woman who tempts us.

Every man wanted her, but he was the one with her toes near his thigh. She extended her leg fully so she could hover at his crotch. Her bare legs were smooth, well muscled with feminine slopes.

Nothing like this spectacle had ever occurred in the Octopus before. Customers stared openly because it was clear that the couple was aware of nobody but each other.

She put her glass down. Her lips parted and glistened, just like pussy ready for cock. The woman had cast a spell over every man in the room. I wanted her at least as desperately as the man she had chosen.

She stroked the inner curve of her breast. As her fingers moved, so did her neckline. Lower, ever lower, inching with excruciating slowness to reveal more of her fleshy tit.

I was so hard I could barely walk. Why had this never happened to *me* at a bar?

The man's erection tented his pants. I felt a mixture of sympathy and jealousy for him.

She stared at him while she stroked her breast. As if she'd willed it, he rose from his seat. His movement did not faze her. In fact, she seemed to expect it. And why not?

He walked by the chair between them. As he approached her, he slid his palm along the outside of her bare thigh. He stopped when her dress bunched at her hip, unable to go any higher. I shuddered with lust at how close his hand was to her glorious ass.

Their eyes locked in some silent contest of wills. She stroked her breast languidly as he caressed her exposed thigh. She moved the fabric at her fingertips so that a full half-moon of her breast rose up into view. He bent down to kiss it.

One of the waiters hooted with delight, which helped to break the thick, awkward silence. Some people laughed nervously, others made valiant attempts to look away. I made no pretense about my interest. I watched shamelessly from only a few meters away. What would she do next?

She removed his hand from her leg but her expression did not change. He returned to his seat with more dignity than most men would have been able to muster. Once he sat, he searched her face, obviously trying to read whether she'd lost interest.

She reached for her purse and my heart sank. Not that I expected them to fuck right there on my bar, but to have this interlude end now, so abruptly, disappointed me beyond words.

The purse was in her lap. She opened it and extracted a key. With the same unwavering gaze, she placed it on the bar and slid it over to him with meaningful deliberateness.

Once he touched it, she got to her feet and glided out of the restaurant. Her tits jiggled provocatively but so subtly as she passed the awed diners. And, oh, that ass. I could practically feel the flesh of her asscheek against my tongue.

Sex is rampant on Greek islands. That any couple should meet and fuck within minutes did not surprise me. But *this* couple. This woman. She would have some kind of plan, I surmised. My curiosity, among other things, needed satisfying. I turned and walked through the kitchen, out the back door and down the alley that led to the street in front of the restaurant. I emerged just after they passed before me.

I followed the man. Indeed, I felt I *was* the man. He, in turn, kept a pace or two behind the woman. She stopped in front of the Stromboli hotel and looked coyly over her shoulder at the man, who nodded with understanding. She walked on and he headed off into the hotel.

Her decorum pleased me. Most Americans did not concern themselves with appearances of modesty or gentility. Most would have just walked into the hotel, leaving the watchful proprietor or other guests to see quite clearly that an assignation was in progress. But this woman knew the proper method was to let him precede her to her room. She would join him shortly, but to anyone watching, the man and the woman were not so obviously together. Impressive, this woman.

Like a fugitive, I lurked by the foliage near her room after the man let himself in. The rooms at Stromboli all open out onto a different patio level carved into the island rock. All of them face the sea.

It was dark, save for the brilliant stars and nearly full moon. I didn't want to frighten the woman when she returned so I crouched behind a small lemon tree and stayed immobile. She arrived minutes later and walked, without fanfare, into her hotel room.

I heard them dissolve into laughter. What was this? Another strange American custom? Sex as comedy? I moved to the window, whose shutters, I noted thankfully, were open.

"I never thought you'd pull it off," the man said, holding her around her waist as he chuckled.

She was giddy, a sharp contrast to her cool demeanor in the restaurant. "What a show that was! Do you suppose they'll ever stop talking about it? I *was* awfully good, wasn't I?" She tossed her streaked auburn hair over her shoulder.

"You seem to think the show is over," he replied, running his hands over her ass.

"Oh, no, my darling. I most certainly am not under that impression."

He raised his eyebrows expectantly as she unbuckled his belt and unzipped his fly. His cock popped out eagerly.

"Why don't you lie down on the bed?" she suggested.

Grinning indulgently, he complied. Pillows propped up his head and he watched her, waiting for direction.

The steely expression returned to her, although now it was tempered with the affection I could see existed between them. Standing at the foot of the bed, she slid her dress over her shoulders and pulled it downward. As she peeled it from her arms and breasts, I saw she wore a white, translucent bra that pushed her tits up and together. It was sheer enough to allow her nipples to show through.

The top half of the dress lay bunched at her waist. She traced the outline of her nipples with her fingertips and he reached for his dick.

"No," she warned.

"What?"

"I don't want you to touch yourself yet."

No Greek man would have permitted a woman to control what he touched in the bedroom! Her impertinence rankled me. And made me harder. But I did not bring a hand to my cock.

She wiggled out of the rest of the dress, letting it pool at her feet. She wore panties unlike anything I'd ever seen: a tiny patch of shimmery fabric at her auburn triangle of hair, and elastic that crossed her hips and disappeared into her ass. I wanted to be that elastic, buried in her ass.

When she was certain he'd had a good look at her soft curves in that fancy lingerie, she walked, still in her heeled sandals, to a nearby suitcase. She pulled out short pieces of rope.

I thought for a moment about leaving. I longed for that rope around my wrists and my ankles.

She attached him to the bed with expert knots. She looped the rope firmly but not tightly. His cock prayed skyward, to the gods, as did mine. Both of us remained clothed and at her mercy.

She crawled up on the bed and knelt between his splayed legs. I wanted her lips on my hot tool. She swirled her tongue around his thickness a few times before she took him into her mouth.

"Oh, Keisha," he moaned.

Her head bobbed up and down in exactly the right rhythm. I pumped my fist with the same tempo, spreading my precome over my shaft and imagining it was her saliva.

The man's eyes were closed and the muscles in his legs tightened. She stopped sucking and straddled him with remarkable agility.

She sat on him, impaled by his engorged cock. There was so little to her panties that entrance to her cunt was unimpeded.

She raised and lowered herself on his pole, moaning with pleasure. Her tits jiggled in the flimsy bra and I wanted her to take it off. *Show me those meaty tits.*

She reached behind her and unhooked the garment. She tore it off and grabbed her own bouncing titties as she rode her lover. What powerful legs this woman had!

It was a small room. The scent of her pussy could not be contained by it. I breathed deeply to enjoy her aroma. My palm was her dripping snatch, enclosing around my cock, sucking it up inside her like a hungry animal. I listened closely and could hear the wet kisses from her juicy hole.

She fucked him faster, harder, landing on him with a force she must have felt all through her cunt. An intensity consumed her so completely that her lover watched her, fascinated.

Her cries came up slowly, as if they started between her legs. They burst loudly from her throat as she bucked and trembled, all the while still bouncing on his cock.

So complete a woman was she that he and I forgot our own gratification. We watched, admired, devoured this orgasmic goddess and let our fluid sit like nitroglycerin in our balls. And we were grateful for the privilege.

When she had let all her orgasms pass through and out of her beautiful body, she fell forward on his chest, nuzzling his neck. I imagined her hot breath in my ear. He kissed her hair, her cheek, her eyes.

"Untie me, babe. I need to fuck your sweet ass."

Yes. Yes, that was exactly what I needed.

Dutifully, she freed him. He immediately sat up and took one of her big tits into his mouth. He sucked like a newborn calf and I licked my lips.

He held her other breast and pushed it up. She bent her head down, stuck out her tongue and lashed at her hard nipple. My knees were weakening at every moment, watching him suck one nipple while she licked the other. My cock swelled in my hand.

A few minutes later, he positioned her with her back to me, by the side of the bed. She bent over and dizziness overtook me. Her perfectly contoured ass was on display for me! The slope of her hips as they melded into her thighs remains a sight I will never forget. I could not decide then or now if I most wanted my face or my cock buried between those rounded cheeks.

The man pulled her silk panties over her hips and down her lovely legs. She stepped out of them. When he positioned him-self behind her, most of my view was obstructed. But he stuffed himself into her pussy quickly enough. He rammed her hard, making her gasp.

"Oh *yes*, Mark! Fuck me, honey. Fuck me, Mark!"

What I could see of her ass shook with each thrust. I was her lover, holding her full hips to steady her against my pounding. He fucked her; I felt her juices coat my balls.

We came at the same time.

With my cock no longer in control, my brain resumed functioning. I grimaced at the sight of my come on the ground, my penis peering at the stars. I saw the American couple cuddle happily on the bed.

And I remembered I had a restaurant to run.

I hurried back to the Octopus, grabbing a tub of fresh *marides* from the back of the restaurant to bring to the front, as if that might explain my disappearance. Every table was full and several parties were waiting. Christos threw me a stern, impatient look.

I busied myself with customers. Business was so brisk that I didn't even notice that Christos had seated the American couple in the corner.

They wore different clothing, more casual and appropriate for a beach climate. They were relaxed and smiling. Even Christos hadn't recognized them, and he waited on them throughout their meal. Oddly, I found I could not face her.

By the time they left, it was nearly midnight. They strolled out, arm in arm, before I went to their table to clear it off.

My heart stopped, then pounded wildly. A room key gleamed on the tablecloth.

Had she left it on purpose? Was this an invitation? Had they seen me and now wanted me to join them? I had no experience in such sophisticated sexual games. My mind raced. I picked up the key and twirled it slowly between my fingers, plotting my escape and my alibi to Christos, when I heard her voice.

"Excuse me."

Her face was before me, so young and fresh, invigorated by good food and good sex.

"Did you perhaps find a key on this table?"

Speechless, I held the small metal object up for her to see. She reached for it, smiling.

"Oh, thank goodness. We were afraid we'd lost it! *Kalinichta!*"

And she disappeared into the night, taking my wildest fantasies with her.

DOWN ON YOUR KNEES

Shanna Germain

Claire believed women could have them. She believed at twelve, when she slid her mother's battered copy of *The Joy of Sex* from beneath the socks in the sock drawer. She believed at fourteen, when she read her older sister's diary, the words that fumbled their way to description. She believed at eighteen, when her best friend Yara emerged, red-faced and smiling, from a make-out session during a party. She had still believed at twenty, on her dorm bed with her third boyfriend's fast and patient fingers trying, trying. But then she stopped believing.

Once, she believed in finding orgasms the way some women believed in finding Jesus. If she just got down on her knees in the name of her savior, she would be rewarded. She visited the church of O whenever she could, believing that some day her prayers would be heard and that hand would come down and bless her. But for all of the time spent on her knees with her head bowed, she never received that ultimate blessing.

It wasn't that sex wasn't good for her—it was, even without orgasm. She liked the buzz in her brain that happened on the dance floor or in that first kiss; loved the way hands crossed her body, soft or hard; craved the smooth slide of a penis into her small spaces. To feel her partner's body tighten just before, the way the toes curled or the ass tightened, she liked that too, knowing she had given them this thing.

For years, it was enough. But now, she is the lamb lost in the desert, wandering without hope. She wants more. Not cuddling or breakfast, but the release she sees in her partners. The sense of ease that lulls them to sleep, or makes them kiss up her neck in groggy pleasure.

Her best friend, Yara, the one who found her orgasm at eighteen, has tried to help. For almost ten years, she's been Claire's orgasm priest: put your hands here, say these words, take the body into your mouth. Claire goes to Yara's house every year for her birthday, her penance and confession. Forgive me mother, for I have not had an orgasm. Every year, Yara gives Claire another vibrator, a new how-to book. Last year, for twenty-nine, Yara gave them both gift certificates for a local have-an-orgasm seminar.

Claire had stared at the tickets in disbelief. "An orgasm class?" she'd said. "What are you going to do, teach?" But she and Yara had gone, and then she'd had to find her labia in the mirror, even though directions weren't her issue. And she'd had to rub her fingers frantically along her drying clit while Yara and the other women earned A-pluses for their Os. It didn't help that the teacher prodded her along with cheerleader yelps that made Claire want to hide under the sex furniture.

This year, on her birthday, Claire doesn't want to talk about sex. She wants to move on to something that doesn't sound like the repetition of dead Latin on her tongue. Her "To-Do Before Thirty" list is unfinished, the word orgasm staring at her in her own youthful purple penmanship. She's done her Hail Marys on the gift of anal beads, flogged herself with the hand-carved paddle Yara had mail ordered, impaled herself with the devil-headed vibrator. All for nothing.

Still, when Yara invites her for her birthday, she goes, and now they are lying sprawled on Yara's red comforter, their feet hanging off the end of the bed. Claire's comfortable here, she knows the oak dresser from Yara's mom, the shag rug, the louvered closet that even now, she knows, harbors some of her own clothes—the jeans that she left here after Yara's twenty-seventh birthday, her blue I'M ONLY A BITCH TO YOU T-shirt that Yara confiscated.

Out in the living room, Yara's current lover, an Icelandic man whose twenty-day visa is expiring, packs his suitcase. Claire is between lovers, or perhaps done with lovers. She can no longer delight in those final, satisfied sighs of others. Or in the way they try, after, with fingers and tongues until she takes their hand or head, and says, "It's okay." It makes her insides feel dry as dirt.

When Yara wiggles closer, her dark curly hair scratches against Claire's cheek, but Claire doesn't move away. Everything is cactus and clay, why not her best friend's hair?

Yara touches Claire's leg with her purple-painted toes. From beneath Yara's pant leg, the bottom half of her tattoo is visible: a swirl of blues and reds. Once Claire thought she might get a tattoo, something with rain and flowers, but now she knows she already has one: her own scarlet O sewn to her chest.

"What do you think?" Yara asks.

Claire knows she means the Icelandic man in the living room, with his chiseled pale skin, like he's been carved from salt and stone. "He seems nice," she says.

"Nice?" Yara asks.

The sides of Claire's nose prickle, like when she used to be able to cry. She rubs her hand across the smooth comforter. There are puckers where the fabric caught on something—who knows what with Yara—and pulled.

Yara's purple-painted toes push hard against Claire's calf. "C'mon, just last week, you would have been *oohing* and *ahhing* over him," she says. "He's just your type."

Yara knows Claire so well—her Icelandic *is* built the way Claire likes, tall and thinly muscled, and that chiseled pale skin. She imagines him above her. She has no qualms about this—she and Yara have shared men before, guys who Yara thinks might help Claire. And, yet, even imagining him beneath her while she kneels over him—her favorite way—she feels nothing. Dry dust settles down her stomach, into the space between her legs.

Yara sits up, turns Claire's face toward her so that Claire can see her eyes, the color of stained wood.

"Oh my," Yara says. "You need an intervention."

Claire's ring catches on the snag in the comforter. She lets it stay there, afraid to pull, unable to find the energy to turn and loosen it. She doesn't want an intervention. She wants to go back in time to that moment before she stopped believing. She wants someone to bring her, not water or wine, but whatever she needs to quench the dull dry air inside her mouth, inside her everywhere. If she had words on her tongue instead of this heavy nothing, she would say how grateful she is for all Yara has done, and then she would crawl under Yara's comforter and sleep until she crumbled into nothing.

"Well, I'd offer you my guy," Yara says. "But I don't think it will help."

Yara drops her hand and face from Claire's. "And here's the truth," she says. "It's his last night here. He leaves for the airport in"— Yara glances at the bedside clock—"an hour. So how's this for a plan? I'm going to fuck him and send him on his way, and then we'll work on you until the wee hours of the morning."

When Yara looks at her, Claire sees that Yara feels guilty for this, like a priest who's abandoned his lost lamb at Christmas mass. Claire isn't sure she understands, but there is so much she doesn't understand that she is able to nod at her friend. Yes, okay. If Yara wants to have an orgasm on her, Claire's, birthday, then so be it. Yara's done as much as anybody, she's done as much as she could. And, really, isn't this what Claire asked for this year? To be left alone in her own dry desert?

"Thank you for this," Yara says, and Claire sees something there in Yara's bottom lip, a small quiver, and that's when she knows—this is the real thing for Yara. The big *L*, the love thing, that other elusive holy grail.

Yara gets off the bed and puts her hands around her mouth, an exaggerated call to arms. "Oh Iceman," she calls. She gives Claire a wink that says, *Remember the days when we were in love with Val Kilmer and Goose and Tom Cruise on his motorcycle?* Claire remembers—she remembers thinking someday she'd have a man like that to make her come.

"Ten minutes," Yara whispers. "Okay, maybe fifteen," and then she leaves Claire in the bedroom with the dresser and the comforter and the closet. Claire listens to Yara's *swish-swish* sound, the way she walks with her pant legs rubbing together, to the Icelander's footsteps across the living room.

"My Yara," he says in his accented voice that matches his chiseled face perfectly.

Claire pulls the corner of the comforter over her head, but it is not enough to block out the sounds of kissing. She would hate Yara if she could, for making her listen to this, for making her wait through it. Through the comforter, still she hears the sounds, even over the crack of her own insides breaking into dust.

Claire realizes the sounds are coming closer. She hears Yara's voice saying, "We can't, Claire's in there," and then her soft laugh, the one she does right before she's about to give in to something.

Claire pulls the comforter off her head in a moment of panic. She's done threesomes before, but never with Yara. Not with Yara. She couldn't bear it if she did it and it didn't work. It would be like seeing the face of God on a piece of toast just before someone covered it in butter.

She'll leave, that's what she'll do. Screw her birthday, and the girl-talk crap. She should have just gone home anyway. But as soon as she's off the bed, they are in the hallway. They aren't in the room yet, but she will never get past without them noticing, without a hassle.

Claire moves toward the far end of the room. The closet doors beckon in their slatted openness. It is pew and confessional both in there, dark and safe. When Claire sees Yara's hand moving in the hallway, she knows now is the time. There will be no other chance to escape.

Claire steps in among the hanging shirts and skirts. When the louvered doors fold closed without a sound, she is grateful for oiled hinges. The closet floor is covered with clothes, but they smell clean at least, like fabric softener and the basil hand cream that Yara wears. Claire kneels on the soft pile, prepared to wait it out. Hanging fabric brushes her shoulders.

Yara and Iceman come into the room, mouths locked. Already, Yara's shirt is unbuttoned and half-slid down her shoulders.

Yara pops the button on Iceman's jeans, even while he leans in and nips at her shoulder, down the side of her arm.

"Where is your friend?" Iceman asks.

Yara breaks the kiss, looks around her room. "I don't know," she says. "She'll be back."

It is not a snide remark. Just Yara's truth. Claire always comes back. Inside the closet, Claire shifts on the clothes, putting her knees on the deepest, softest part of the pile. She feels safe in here, watching from the dark space. No one sees her, no one is waiting to see if she'll finally come.

Yara slides the jeans down over his thin, muscled hips. The fabric falls to his ankles. It is only when he lifts one leg to step out of them that Claire realizes he wasn't wearing underwear. His cock, as thin and long as the rest of him, is already hard, curling up like a smile.

"I can't believe you're leaving," Yara says, even as she hooks her thumbs inside her jeans and her baby blue thong, pulls them down in one easy motion. Her thigh sports a new tattoo, a gold-yellow sunshine as big as Claire's fist. "You're going to have to fuck me"—Yara pantomimes with her hands—"the way we did last night."

Iceman smiles. His smile *is* the same shape as his cock. It makes Claire want to laugh, but she drops her head down, looks at the pile of shoes in the corner until she doesn't want to laugh anymore.

When she looks up, Iceman has his hands on Yara's face. His thumb runs across the mole on her jawline.

"Yara," he says, and his voice sounds like prayer.

The thing that comes over Claire is as sudden and hot as the tears. She reaches out, wipes the wet on something hanging in front of her. The fabric is soft and smells like fresh-cut grass. She is stupid, stupid for letting Yara lead her by the hand, stupid for being here. When she leaves the closet, she will find new friends, she will get herself a boyfriend and be happy for his orgasms. Or she will meditate and do Upside-Down Dog until her head spins and her clit dries up and falls off.

When Claire looks back up, Yara is naked. Claire sees she's shaved since last year's orgasm class, a small thin strip of hair the only thing guiding the way. Claire's own bush is ridiculous, she knows, outgrown and untended. How can something grow in such dryness? She puts her hand down the front of her jeans, pulls the long, kinky hairs. No one sees it anyway.

Iceman pulls his shirt over his head. His chest muscles are biteable, hard but not too hard. Claire shuts her eyes against the ache that trickles down her belly. But she can't resist watching, to see how they fucked last night, to see what this man will do with his thin cock and his long fingers.

When Yara crouches down, hands and knees on the carpet, she faces Claire. If she looked up, she would see Claire through the slats in the closet, Claire is sure of it, but Yara doesn't look up, she looks down at the carpet. Yara goes down on her elbows, so that her ass is in the air. She is curvy in the way that looks right in this position, like someone should paint her here. *Orgasming Girl on Carpet.*

From behind, Iceman goes down on his knees. He runs his hands over the fleshy curves of Yara's ass. Then he leans down further, gives the side of her leg a nip. Yara squeals, and then her voice settles down into a low grunt as he moves further and further toward her center. Claire can only see the top of his head over Yara's ass, but she knows, she knows by the way Yara sounds, when he hits the spot.

Claire's face is mashed up as close as it will get to the closet doors without touching the wood. Her hand still pulls at her curls, and when she reaches down, she's surprised to find that in her own deep center, she is wet. Dripping even. She can't remember the last time she didn't need lube to run her fingers across her clit like this, slow and quiet, so quiet they won't hear her, so quiet she can pretend she's not even doing it. She wants to unbutton her jeans, but she is afraid to break this moment, so she just spreads her legs a little wider on the pile of clothes.

Outside the closet, Iceman's head rises and falls behind Yara's ass. Yara pants a little, rocks back and forth on her elbows and knees. Her nipples rub on the carpet, tight and pink. Claire reaches up with her other hand, inside her shirt and bra, and pinches her own nipple until it hardens beneath her fingers. Pain and pleasure light her up from nipple to clit. A new wetness floods her fingers.

"Wait," Yara says, and she moves away from Iceman, up on her knees. "I want to be on top," she says.

They switch, until Iceman is beneath her, his head so close to Claire's closet that she can see a few dark strands in his pale hair. Lying down, he is long and lean, only his cock rising up like a slanting steeple from his hips. Yara kneels above him and puts her hand on his cock. When she makes a fist around him and pumps, he raises his hips off the floor, moves toward her. Yara lowers herself onto him, slow, slow. Claire watches his cock slide inside her, a half inch at a time, disappearing until there is only hip and hip, moving in unison. Yara pinches her nipples into long pink points. She leans back a little, gives Iceman space to fit his fingers to her clit.

Claire's clit aches, and one hand is not enough anymore. She unbuttons her pants, slides both hands inside her wet curls. Claire's fingers are frantic across her own slippery clit, matching Iceman's strokes. She's so caught up in the watching that she forgets her fingers are moving, until she feels the familiar ache in her wrist. Even then, she doesn't stop, just changes angles without looking away. Watching is good, she realizes, but it is the *not* being watched that is better. This is what she is meant to do, to offer up her silent, fingering prayer in the dark confessional of spaces.

Through the slats in the closet, Claire watches as Yara leans back further, grabs her heels with her hands. Beneath her, Iceman pumps into her and rubs his hand across her clit. Yara's eyes are on the closet doors now, but they don't see Claire, they've gone somewhere else, they're seeing the thing that Claire wants to see.

In the small, dark space, some strange thing possesses Claire, rushing out from her clit in waves of heat and light. She feels like a star must feel before it explodes. Claire's body is no longer her own. She gives it up willingly to whatever higher being there is. When Iceman flicks his fingers against Yara's clit, Claire's clit throbs. When Yara moans, Claire's mouth opens. When Yara clenches around Iceman's cock, Claire sticks two fingers inside herself, rocks back and forth. And when Yara comes, grunting on top of Iceman, her head thrown back, legs shaking, Claire comes too, her fingers flames against the water of her clit, burning and quenching. Finally, Claire knows possession, salvation, light. Claire believes.

LATE BLOOMER

Alison Tyler

I can actually see things from Nina's point of view. It's taken me a solid ten years, but I finally understand. Nina thought I was too tightly wound. She wanted to shake me to my core, and she did a damn fine job. Now, a decade after the fact, I have come to appreciate her style, her dead-on sense of timing. As well as her unbelievable ass.

There she stood, in the center of my sunken living room, stark naked and unabashedly gorgeous, her tanned skin gleaming, blonde hair like liquid amber spilling out down her back. She arched her hips ever so subtly, so that her rear end looked enticingly biteable. I could imagine taking a few short steps forward, going on my knees, sinking my teeth into those delicately rounded cheeks. Then she spun around slowly, watching herself the entire time in the mirror that hung over the fireplace mantel, looking over her shoulder to catch herself from every luscious angle. A former cheerleader, Nina had a way of moving as if she always knew that eyes were on her—and generally, they were.

But they weren't on me.

I was the quintessential wallflower, the late bloomer—one who hadn't yet bloomed at all. Supremely self-conscious in my womanly body, I worked in pathetic desperation to hide every evidence of my feminine curves. My uniform was simple: well-worn jeans and baggy sweaters, sleeves dangling down past my wrists. I used my fingers to occasionally push my thick dark hair out of my eyes, but generally I hid behind my long bangs, safe in my mantra that nobody cares what writers look like.

While Nina preened, I leaned against the doorjamb between the living room and the dining room, clad in my beloved ancient navy blue sweats and an oversized man's T-shirt. My brown hair was tangled, twisted into snakelike coiled curls, and my eyes were tired from hours spent staring at the computer screen. I cradled a cup of coffee tightly between both hands, as if it was my security blanket, but I knew that I wouldn't feel truly awake until the third cup had kicked in. My best work happens late into the night. Still I stared, unable to tear myself away. Nina's radiance captivated me. There was no way I would be able to go about my daily routine knowing that she was prancing around the apartment in her birthday suit. How could I possibly concentrate?

"I'm the only one who can do this," she crowed at me, still admiring her own breathtaking reflection.

"Naked yoga?" I asked, nonplused as she began her standard Sun Salutation, slender arms lifted high to the ceiling. I started to drink the coffee quickly even though it was too hot. My burned tongue woke me up a little bit faster.

"No, Melanie," she said with a sly smile, "walk around the house in my altogether." Now she grinned, her palms pressed flat together, and assumed a pose of total serenity. I stared at the delicate lines of muscles in her back, the tattoo of a violet rose blossoming at the base of her spine. "*You* wouldn't want Joe to see you undressed, and he has no desire for you to catch him in the buff. But *I'm* free to do as I please."

She was right. Joe and I were roommates. That's all. We'd never experienced even the tiniest spark of sexual intrigue between us. Not even when drunk. The thought of him seeing me naked made me want to hide under my heavy down duvet for a month. I could just imagine what he would think of me, with my Medusa curls, dark features, bee-stung lips, bad-girl hips.

Joe liked the starlets, slim-waisted girls with ironed blonde hair and the type of iris-blue eyes that only come from a colored contact lens kit. A wannabe screenwriter, he didn't buy into my belief that writers can look like shit and still be successful. He spent hours at the gym, creating the most sellable physique, as if his tight abs would make his lackluster screenplays any better.

Nina was my best friend from high school. And she was fucking him. She didn't care if I saw her without her clothes on, because I'd been seeing her naked for years—in department store dressing rooms as we tried on outfits for prom (hers a slinky bombshell number, mine long-sleeved and solid black), in swimming pool changing rooms as we slid into our suits (me in a safe, cover-all one-piece, Nina in a leopard-print bikini), and in slumber party bedrooms as we put on night clothes and gossiped about boys. (And yes, she was in a sheer baby-doll, while I was in plaid flannels. And *yes*, she was the one doing the gossiping while I listened carefully, storing away every sordid detail.)

She had no fear of being exposed—hell, she reveled in it— and now, the second week after she'd moved into my apartment, she was driving this fact home every single day. When I came in from the grocery store, there she'd be: naked. When I stumbled down the hallway in the morning in desperate need of coffee, there she'd be: naked.

Joe liked it. What guy wouldn't want his current femme fatale to show her goodies whenever possible? He was a man, after all, and I could tell exactly how much he enjoyed her exhibitionist qualities from the glow in his pale green eyes whenever he caught her parading around the kitchen. He chuckled and patted her ass possessively when he discovered her cooking in a little lace apron, high-heeled stripper shoes, and nothing else. When I was present, he made polite yet faux attempts to get her back into her clothes—"Come on, Nina, we have company"— as if I were a guest in my own fucking house, but we all knew that watching her in the buff made him a very happy—as well as very horny—man.

Besides, all of this was my own damn fault, so I couldn't possibly complain. I'd invited Nina to come stay with me for a minivacation, and she'd hit it off with Joe that very first night. We'd all gone out for drinks at the Snake Pit on Melrose, and I'd watched Nina slip closer and closer to Joe in the red vinyl booth as the evening progressed. In between strolls down memory lane, she'd teased him with her body, running her fingertips along the delicate line of her neck, or setting one hand on his. Just for a moment. Just long enough.

"Mel was always a wallflower," Nina told him at one point when she was flashing back to our high school days. "You should have seen her at the dances, pressed flat against the wall, staring."

"Taking notes," Joe grinned, nodding. "Melanie's always writing stuff down." He didn't mean offense by the comment; I could tell. He was simply adding to the conversation.

"She just watched." Nina met my eyes. I wondered what she saw there.

"But I'll bet *you* were dancing," Joe said to Nina, both appreciatively and correctly. "I'll bet you were the belle of the ball." His hand slipped under the table, and I was sure it had come to rest on her inner thigh.

Ultimately, she'd practically been in his lap, and nausea had swirled over me as I watched the two kiss. One of his big hands found the back of her head and pulled her forward. The heat between them made me ache. When they parted, her cranberry-hued lipstick had smeared his mouth, and she used her thumb to rub the stain away, touching his face with a sense of ownership.

I didn't want Joe—believe me when I say that I didn't. Burly former football players have never done anything for me. But I wanted what Nina had, the confidence that shone through even when she was dressed simply, in a formfitting white T-shirt and stovepipe indigo jeans. The power that emanated from her as she gripped her bottle of Heineken and took a swig. Even in L.A., the land of the beautiful, Nina stood out, the same way she had in high school—at the pool or at the prom. I faded into the background then, as I faded at the Snake Pit. A wallflower in a garden of championship roses.

Nina and Joe stayed to close the bar. I don't think they even noticed when I put my money on the table and left the Pit, heading home on my own in the darkness. Much later, I heard them trying to be quiet as they stumbled back into the apartment, and then heard them forgetting about trying to be quiet, in his room, fucking against the wall. I listened, because I couldn't help myself, as she moaned his name: "God, Joe. Oh, my fucking god—"

He wasn't as audible as she was. I pressed my ear harder against the cold wall, devouring every sound. He was breathing heavily, nearly panting, and repeating her name, but she was doing most of the talking. Telling him what she wanted. Giving him naughty little commands. "Do it like this. Come on, Joe. Harder—"

I thought of her arched over the bed, with Joe in the rear. Thought of what harder meant. She wanted him to slam into her. She wanted to really feel it. I didn't have to close my eyes to envision the scene. A movie played out on the wall before me with hardly any assistance at all. I'd seen Nina naked often enough to know exactly what she looked like now, cast in the most erotic positions as Joe, big hulking stud that he was, took care of her.

They started near the bed. I could hear the mattress springs squeaking, and I visualized Joe fucking her from the rear, her jeans down, panties to the side. They were in a hurry, and a bit hazy from the alcohol, and they went at it like animals. I could hear him crooning to her—"Nina, pretty Nina"—and my high school chum taking charge, as she always did.

"Don't come. Not yet. Let's do it like this—"

There was the sound of confusion, and I realized that one of them had knocked something over in their rush. It wouldn't have been Nina. Even drunk, she was graceful. Was she performing a striptease? Of course she was. Joe must have been mesmerized, watching as she tossed her shirt across the room, then her bra; then peeled her jeans all the way off, before hooking her thumbs under the ribbonlike band of her teeny-tiny thong and slipping it down her slender thighs.

"Against the wall," she told him. "Fuck me right there—"

All of those hours at the gym paid off for Joe. He had stamina. He could lift her clear off the ground, press her up against the wall, and fuck her nonstop until she creamed. And he did. I mimicked her position on the other side, my whole body sealed to the plaster, becoming one third of their nonconsensual ménage à trois, reveling in the sensation of being a participant, even an invisible one.

Joe thrust into her, and I contracted on an invisible cock. Joe said, "Look at me," and I opened my eyes wide, as if he were speaking to me. When Nina made noise, it was as if I could *feel* her moans. As if I were the one making those noises. I saw two visions in my head—Joe fucking Nina against the wall, and Nina slow dancing with partner after partner in the dimly lit gymnasium back in high school.

She was right—about what she told Joe at the bar. All I ever did *was* watch. But I wasn't watching now. I was listening. Somehow it was even better. At least, at first it was.

"Oh, yes, Joe," she purred. "Just like that. Now touch my clit. Use your hand on it. Rub it, Joe. Rub my clit faster. Faster—"

He must have been doing everything that she asked, because she started to go hoarse, her voice gone, her words fading to groans. I bit my lip and closed my eyes tight, feeling the climax build deep within me. Feeling as if *I* were the one being fucked. Nina found it in herself to scream as she came, and I thrust one palm against my mouth, bit into the tender skin there to keep myself from echoing her wild, untamed noise.

After making Nina come the first time, Joe seemed to find his own sense of power. Suddenly, he was speaking. "You like that?"

"Mmm-hmmm."

"Bad girl—" Joe said. "Bossing me around like that. Telling me what to do."

"You think I'm a bad girl?"

"I *know* you are."

"So what are you going to do about it?"

He didn't answer verbally. Instead, I heard him telling her to get into the proper position.

"Position?"

"You heard me, Nina. You know what I mean."

There was a low giggle, sexy as hell, and then I heard her say, "Like this?"

"You think I'm kidding. You think I'm being funny—"

And seconds later, I heard him spanking her, could tell immediately what those sexy sounds were, the erotic slapping sounds of skin on skin, and once more I could see the movie in my mind—petite blonde Nina upended over Joe's sturdy lap, his firm hand on her ass, connecting hard. Was he punishing her for turning his world upside down? Or did he understand somehow that this scene wasn't solely for him and Nina? It was for me, too. Because Nina knew all of my little fantasies. She knew that being spanked was the ultimate turn-on for me, knew that watching—watching people together—floored me like nothing else. Best friends share secrets. But did she think she was giving me a gift here? Or was she showing off yet again?

Without a thought as to what might happen if I got caught, I moved away from the wall, slid silently out of my bedroom, and padded quietly down the hall. As I'd expected, the door to Joe's room was open. Only a sliver, but enough. I walked toward the open doorway as softly as I could, but I probably needn't have bothered. They were busy, consumed by their own actions. They didn't notice when I made my way right outside his bedroom door, positioning myself so that I could see Nina, ass upward, and Joe, spanking her hard.

The fact that the door was ajar wasn't too surprising. Nina was always a proud exhibitionist. At parties, she made sure to be seen kissing the cutest guy center stage, letting him put his hand up her top or down her skirt, closing her eyes as she became the pure definition of ecstasy. She didn't think being on display made her look like a slut—she thought it made her look wanted. In demand.

Once, when we were on a double date together at a drive-in,

she actually made love in the backseat with her lucky man of the moment. I held my breath as I stared at the screen through the front window, not seeing the movie at all, captivated instead by the sultry noises coming from the backseat. First the wet sounds of Nina delivering a world-class blow job, slurping sounds punctuated by the moans of her man. Then the undeniable noises of her slipping onto his lap and pumping her body until she reached her own personal Nirvana. My date stared straight forward, too, realizing from the start that he was going nowhere with me. Not that he would have wanted to. I was in head-to-toe black, hair in my face, as always. Nina was in a sunburst sundress, low in the back, low in the front.

There was nothing Nina ever found too revealing.

Good, I thought as I watched Joe's hand make sweet contact with her sublime ass. *Spank her harder. Spank her for me.*

Joe and I had been roommates for nearly a year, and I was aware when he brought women home, those one-dimensional paper dolls who all left the same sort of lilting messages on our answering machine afterward. "Joe? It's Angela?" Always with an upturn at the end. A question as if they weren't quite sure who they were or what they wanted from him. But I'd never heard him involved in anything like this before, never thought to go spy on him when he was in bed with one of his candy girls. Truthfully, I'd never given what he did in bed all that much thought. This was different. Nina's climax was so powerful I could practically taste her pleasure, and it was with a dark, thrilling wave of guilt that I retreated back down the hall to my own futon bed and stroked myself to a much quieter orgasm of my own, picturing the scene in an endless, X-rated loop.

In the morning, Nina strolled into my bedroom wearing one of Joe's old oversized football jerseys and a Cheshire grin.

"Thanks," she said, smiling coyly at me.

"For—?"

"The invitation."

I was silent, hearing a response in my head but not able to voice the words. I'd invited her to stay with me, not to screw my roommate. But that sounded bitter, didn't it? Was I always bitter around Nina? When she wasn't close by, I had my own form of confidence, didn't I? I stood behind my work. My stories spoke for me. Didn't matter that my closet was a sea of black. That my shoes looked like men's shoes. That dressing up to me meant putting on black slacks rather than black jeans. When Nina wasn't there, I was witty and sly.

Nina looked around my room, her large eyes carefully appraising my desk, my computer, the art on my walls. She didn't say a word, but I could hear her judging, and I felt a competitive urge swell within me. We had been best friends since junior high school, but rivals, as well. The feeling was one that I thought we'd overcome after college, jobs, real life. It was one of the reasons I'd invited her to stay—to show her that I didn't care anymore. Didn't care that she was prettier, sleeker, more exciting.

What a fucking lie.

There it was. Hitting me hard in the gut. I didn't want Joe, so what did it matter that she was sleeping with him? I couldn't answer that. And why had she come? Maybe Nina was my friend because being near me made her look even more luscious. Compared to my drab outfits and downcast eyes, she was a vision of radiance. But why was I her friend? Because she showed me what life would be like if I took a risk? Because she had the guts to, to—

Without a pause, she whipped off the shirt and headed naked to the bathroom to take a shower, giving me a glimpse of her perfect bubble butt and the subtle plum-hued handprints that still decorated it.

Only a week, I told myself. *Then she'll be gone.*

But she wasn't. In she moved. And naked she remained.

She did the crossword puzzle in the dining room, naked with her feet tucked up under her. She showered with the door open. She washed the dishes in her birthday suit. If she could have gone to work naked, I'm sure she would have. But for the first month and a half, she didn't have a job, and therefore, she had no need of clothes.

Paranoid, I decided that she was behaving like this only to mess with me. Perhaps she was fucking Joe—but she was head-fucking me. I mean, wouldn't she get cold at some point? Want to slip on some fuzzy kneesocks, a comfy sweatshirt? No. She turned up the heat, and continued to revel in her altogether.

And I hated her for it.

The funny thing is that even back then I knew what I should have done. I should have taken my own clothes off, should have stripped down on that first day and done naked yoga at her side. Nina wouldn't have been able to stop me. It was *my* apartment, too, as well as Joe's. What could they have done about it?

Instead, I grew distant and shadowy. I lurked around the rooms, sidling into the kitchen when I knew they were in the living room. Rushing to get out of the apartment in the morning. Drinking my coffee at King's Road Cafe rather than in my own kitchen. I felt storm-cloud gray compared to Nina's golden beams of light, felt weighted down and heavy, listening every evening to their X-rated activities through the thin walls.

"From behind, Joe," Nina would tell him, her voice so urgent. "Take me from behind tonight."

And I'd be in there with them, my head against the wall, sickly drinking in every seductive moment, no longer retreating to my bed to get off, but touching myself right there. Standing. A wallflower for real. One that only bloomed at night.

He spanked her at the end of every session. He reddened her ass until she cried, and the thought of her tears made me come harder than I ever had.

As the weeks went on, I began wearing more, as if to compensate for Nina's lack of garments. I added a zippered hoodie to my standard at-home wardrobe of T-shirts and sweats, slid a blue-and-green-plaid flannel robe on top of that, looked as if I were heading out to the Arctic when I was only walking down the hall.

I would have worn clothes in the shower, if I could have. Would have put on galoshes, thick kneesocks, gloves, shin guards, my skin disappearing under layer upon layer of protective gear. Until one morning I caught my reflection in the bathroom mirror. I had on a black-and-gray-striped wool hat pulled low over my forehead as I was brushing my teeth, and I met my reflection and shook my head. What had happened to me? Where the hell was I?

I moved out the next day. And it was like moving from a cold winter in North Dakota to the island tropics. I rented a sun-filled apartment near Venice Beach and shed my clothes as if they were on fire.

But it took years for me to shed the rest of my inhibitions.

Only over time have my clothes grown smaller to fit my actual body. Only after many forays out to the beach have I traded in my safe one-pieces and long-sleeved cover-ups for bright bikinis.

Wallflowers are made, not born. That's what I've learned. And maybe *flower* isn't the right term, after all. Maybe *wall bud* is more correct. All the girls pressed tightly to the wall have the potential to bloom someday. They can step forward, turn their heads up to the sun, feel the heat rush over them.

That's why I pack light when I go to visit Nina and Joe. They got married, if you can believe it. A vacation romance turned into the real thing. Got married and quit the L.A. scene. Moved to Oregon, where he fixes cars and she works nights in a local café. And when they meet me at the airport, I can't help but grin as he lifts my suitcase.

"Not much here," Joe says. "You're traveling light."

When he says the words, he's staring at me, and I can tell that he appreciates the way I look. I've lost the last of the puppy fat that hounded me through high school and college, learned to appreciate yoga as well, streamlining my figure as well as my attitude. Just dropping my extra heavy garments made me look as if I'd shed twelve pounds.

I shake my head and Nina catches my eye, but I don't say a word. They're different now. Her hair is cut short—not hip, just no-nonsense—and the color looks dull and flat, not so much like gold as straw. Joe's got a hard gut that he didn't have in Los Angeles, and there's more than a hint of gray in his dark hair. I feel sleek and confident as we head to their car. I'm invited for a week, but I'm only staying for one night.

It's all I need.

Joe sets my suitcase down in the guest room and heads outside to start the grill. I look at my reflection in the mirror on the back of the closet door—we're all older, but late bloomers look different from those who peak too early. Late bloomers get theirs in the second act.

My body is slim and fit, my dark eyes are bright.

It's taken me ten years to get here, to see where Nina was coming from. But now, I can look back and smile as I kick off my boots and jeans, then pull my long-sleeved black shirt over my head and get ready to walk naked down the hall.

SHARING THE PERFECT COCK

Rachel Kramer Bussel

My boyfriend, Kyle, has the perfect cock. Really—if there were cock models, the way there are hand and feet models, I bet he'd be making a fortune off his pecker. It's tall and poised and beautiful, sleek and strong, with light brown hairs curling at the base, as if a proud statue were rising from a vineyard. The first time I saw it I almost wept, but I resisted—and quickly got down on my knees. I've worshipped his dick, literally, since day (or rather, night) one and am just as smitten with the member as the man even ten years down the road. Don't worry, he's equally as enthralled with my pussy, and together we've had countless sexual adventures. But lately, I've come to the conclusion that his package really is too perfect not to share. I mean, what kind of selfish, spoiled brat would I be if I kept such a gorgeous cock all to myself?

Okay, you've got me. I'm the consummate selfish, spoiled brat, and I want to share his dick because I want to watch. I've been going wild picturing another girl's lips wrapped around that luscious fat head, her saliva dripping down his dick as she opens wide and takes him inside while he looks on proudly, brushing her hair from her face. I want to see everything I don't get to see when I'm lying on my stomach, ass in the air, taking a pounding from him as his cock smoothly dives inside me, my G-spot rushing toward him, my hips undulating beneath him, my body his for the taking; everything I don't get to see when his cock's all the way down my throat and I'm in blow-job heaven. Just thinking about his cock makes me horny, but usually I have it buried inside me, somewhere, swelling to fit my entire mouth, cunt or ass, his hard length leaving me little room to think or look; I must simply feel him grinding against my sensitive flesh until he rings me dry—or, wet.

I haven't told him yet, but I've been on a mission, a hunt. Every hot girl who passes my way, whether it's the waitress at our local vegetarian joint, with her long braided pigtails and ripped denim skirt and camouflage shirt that just hints at the curves underneath, or my boss's slamming secretary who I swear could make a killing as a stripper. She has flaming red hair, perfectly pink lips that she keeps natural or just hinting of gloss, and she wears these business suits that manage to be sexier than a bikini, her tits and ass practically popping out of their pinstripes. She gets away with her wild collection of stockings, in various hues with patterns and designs that could make even this confirmed straight girl lean down and worship my way from her feet on up. One time she even came back from a trip to England with black tights emblazoned with the Fab Four on them. Thankfully, our ad agency is pretty open to experimental dressers. She's never been anything but efficient and friendly, yet sometimes I detect a glimmer of something deeper, a womanly, sensual swirl to her hips; a gleam in her eyes that tells me she'd be perfect splayed across our bed with Kyle's cock spearing her over and over. But I know how badly that could go, so I move on.

In the end, Carrie, the girl who will grant me a front-row seat at my very own private sex show starring my boyfriend's dick and a beautiful babe, finds me. We meet at the gym, where she beckons me over so I can help her lift those last five pounds of a monstrous weight that I'm shocked her tiny body can handle. When she gets up, panting and exerted, instead of sticking out her hand for me to shake, she flexes her bicep, showing me just how strong—and sexy—she really is. Then she grants me a dazzling grin, showing off not just perfect even white teeth, but that the feeling is genuine, lighting up her whole face. I'd follow her anywhere if she'd give me another smile like that, and I know Kyle would too. We spend the rest of our workout time in close proximity, and I grunt extra hard as I push the weights with my legs, in part because my pussy is throbbing from my thinking about her sliding all over my boyfriend, brushing her breasts against his chest, her pussy hovering over his cock or his mouth, teasing him until he begs for mercy.

I know it might sound weird to you, but I don't want a threesome. While fun for other people, they've always seemed to me like too much work without enough reward—exciting, but not nearly as much so as watching this gorgeous woman devour every inch of Kyle. I want to watch him as I've never gotten to see him, his cock standing tall, his body at its most vulnerable as he strains toward her. I don't waste much time before bringing up the topic—unlike the rest of the gym-goers, who huddle around the juice bar for a dark green kale-filled smoothie, we head to a real bar, and over massive margaritas, I start to gush about my sexy man. I even whip out my favorite photo of him wearing just shorts on the beach in Hawaii, his skin tan and gleaming, his erection faintly visible, if you're looking. She licks the salt around the rim of her glass, then brings her tiny tongue back into her mouth and sucks. "He's quite the hunk—you're a lucky girl, Sarah," she says.

"You know, you could be lucky too," I say, taking a big sip from the light green slush.

"I don't seem to meet guys like that, no matter how hard I try," she replies, her voice slightly wistful as her eyes focus on something far away, or far behind.

"No, I mean..." I trail off, putting one hand on her leg, lightly, as the words come to me. "You can share his cock with me." I look away for a minute, my cheeks burning even as I'm determined to share my fantasy with her. "I have this thing where I want to watch him with another girl. He's the hottest guy I've ever been with, and I just feel like his dick is too perfect to keep all to myself. We've been together, and faithful, for ten years. Believe me, he doesn't even know about this naughty little fantasy of mine, though I'm pretty sure he'll agree to it in a snap—especially if you're involved. What's not to like? He'll get to fuck a beautiful girl, you'll get to enjoy what truly is the finest cock I've ever seen, and I'll get...well, I'll get to watch." I say "watch" like I'm winning the lottery or diving into an ocean of chocolate, like watching her and him together will be the pinnacle of my life thus far—and I mean it.

She drains her glass, her eyes seeking mine, making sure I'm for real. "But...why?" she asks, more confused than disdainful.

"I don't even really know. It's not like it just occurred to me today. I've been having dreams where I'm lying in bed and he's on his back and some beautiful girl is moving all around him, exactly the same way I do. I start telling her how he likes his dick sucked, but then I realize she's got it under control." I pause, searching her face. "I know, most women would die of jealousy if their guy so much as kissed another girl, but I'm freaky like that. You can't have him, but I'd love it if you borrowed him for a night," I finish, not sure what she'll say.

"Can I see it?" she asks finally, after a silence during which I try to look anywhere but at her. The bartender refreshes our glasses, and I fill my mouth with the icy drink before replying.

"His cock? Sure—I'll email you a photo when I get home." I lean in close, pushing her hair back as I let my lips brush lightly against her ear, getting a bit of a shock as I do so. "Your mouth's going to water when you see it, I promise."

Carrie looks like she's trying to figure out what to say as she licks the newly salted rim of her glass. "Girl, I have to tell you, I think you're a little bit crazy. But so am I, and he looks so fine, I feel like I'd be kicking myself if I refused. He really doesn't know a thing about this yet?" she asks, her voice lilting upward.

"Not yet, but he will," I say, slipping her my card as she scrawls her information on a napkin.

We finish our drinks, but every time her tongue pokes out to lick the glass, I can't help picturing it winding its way along his cock. I'm ready to race home, and I do—right after she leaves, right after I sneak off to the bar's bathroom and bring myself to a quick, rousing orgasm as my fingers flick at my wet clit while my other hand muffles my moans.

When I get home, I find Kyle on the couch in front of a football game. I smile and say, "Hey, baby," but when he puts his arms out to welcome me, I instead reach down and grab his cock, sinking to my knees. I pull down the layers of his shorts and boxers to unveil a dick that's already half-hard and getting harder by the minute as I hold it. I lean forward and ever-so-lightly suck the head into my mouth, then sit back and let my tongue toy with the veins traveling up and down his shaft before pulling back to look up at him. I'm gratified to see his eyes glued on my face.

"To what do I owe this honor?" he asks, his face lined with sexy stubble, his light brown eyes glinting as he tries not to break out into a grin.

"To a girl—Carrie," I say, then go right back for another lick. He moans as I inch my lips downward, taking half of his length into my mouth, but knowing he's not done growing. "I'm going to show her how to do this," I tell him, breaking my mouth's grip momentarily before plunging back down in one smooth movement, my lips wrapped around my teeth as I feel his cock travel all the way down my throat. I keep his full length inside me for as long as I can, breathing in his manly scent, feeling every bit of him pressing against my lips, my cheeks; surrounded by cock, cock, and more cock. Finally I slide slowly, reluctantly upward, my cheeks already aching with that glorious effort my blow jobs entail.

"What?" he asks, his voice husky, his eyes slightly cloudy as I stand and then straddle him, his naked cock bouncing back against him, then getting flattened between us as I rub my pussy along his hardness.

"I'm going to give her a little show and tell, and then she's gonna fuck you and suck your cock while I watch. I'm gonna make sure she does it perfectly," I say, then quickly plant my mouth back on his pole, tasting my own heady juices. The whole scenario, from the feel of his hot penis in my mouth to picturing Carrie doing the very same thing, to his strangled moans, has me soaking wet. When he pulls me up toward him, turning me around so my hips are hovering over his face, then starts to devour me as I swallow him, I relent, even though normally I prefer to do one thing at a time, fully savoring each sensation. As his tongue parts my lower lips, diving into my swollen, dripping sex, I shudder all over, my hard nipples mashed against his torso, my mouth slackening involuntarily as he pushes deeper inside. His hot tongue swirls in mesmerizing circles as I sink my lips down, down, down, until they meet the base of his cock, the head easing around the bend in my throat. His fingers ply my clit, parting the hood and massaging the hard button beneath as his tongue probes me, his lips and teeth and fingers making me rumble. I ease up on his cock, barely able to breathe, barely wanting to. When he adds a finger inside me alongside his tongue, I'm a goner, my entire lower half tightening and then sparking, my legs clamped around his head as I suck the crown of his dick for all I'm worth, rewarded by the hot spurts of come that erupt from him.

He kisses me between my legs a few more times and then we finally turn around, and I taste myself, this time on his lips. Kyle looks into my eyes, smoothing my hair off my sweaty forehead, his fingers tracing my brows. "I'll give you anything you want, but I have to tell you, I don't think any girl out there can suck my cock the way you do," he finally says.

"Just wait," I tease, my previously sated body already perking up again at the thought of Carrie grinding herself against my man. I move aside, looking up and down at the man I consider my personal male model, my own private piece of eye candy others may sometimes get to borrow as their eyes drink their fill while we walk down the street, but who I get to take home every night. Feeling him against me is still a thrill, a prize, a treasure, but sharing him is going to take things to a whole new level.

I just hope Carrie is as excited as I am. When I call her the next day to follow up on the photo of Kyle's cock I'd sent her, she tells me she had a dream about him, about us. "I was lying on my back, my hands above my head, and his dick was coming at me, so big and hard and powerful. I spread my legs at the same time I opened my lips and he entered me in one fast motion. I gripped the headboard, and pulled against it, and then you shackled me to it so I really couldn't move, and while he fucked my face I watched his cock as it moved in and out. Then I saw you, naked, with your fingers between your legs, and I tried to focus on sucking his dick while memorizing the way you were touching yourself so I could do it later." Her words spill out in one big outpouring, racing ahead of one another, tripping over themselves in her eagerness to share her fantasy with me. The more she talks, the wetter I get, picturing exactly what she's described.

"I guess that means you're in," I tease her, knowing that I'd have a fight on my hands if I tried to refuse her at this point.

After that, everything else moves at warp speed. For the next few days, all I can think about is watching Kyle and Carrie, directing them in my own little play, and the very idea of her naked along with him, in a scene that I'd created but ultimately would only be a bit player in, has the part of my stomach closest to my pussy doing somersaults, dropping as far as it does when I ride a roller coaster. My body literally aches, and the night before we're to meet, when Kyle slides a simple finger inside me, I pitch forward, burying my face in his shoulder as I clutch him, my eyes tight as I squirm. "You're thinking about me with her, aren't you, Sarah? I know you are, and damn it, now I am too. You've made me want to fuck another woman, even though I'm doing it for you," he says, his voice rough, almost growling, as his finger surrenders to my cunt's entreaties, pushing as far as it can go while the flat of his hand mashes my clit. "I'm gonna enjoy it. I'm gonna shove my tongue so deep inside her cunt that she'll scream." I reach for his cock through the haze, each of us alternating a fantasy web with our dream girl.

But as many scenarios as we've played out the night before, none of them could have prepared us for how hungry Carrie is for him. Any reservations she may have had have clearly vanished, because she pounces on my man immediately, as if they've been the ones conducting the secret affair, negotiating this night under cover of darkness, not her and me. I'm wearing a silky sheer black camisole and the tiniest scrap of black lace panties, which are soaked practically from the moment I put them on. I've kept them on me, though, letting my scent permeate the room, dipping my fingers inside to offer Kyle a taste of my juices as we wait. Then, all too soon, she's here, looking even hotter than she did when we met, au naturel in a slinky red dress that seems molded to her body. We converge in the living room where she greets me with a full body hug, her hands traveling from my shoulders on down, and then I hear her say, "And you must be Kyle." Unconsciously, I slip away, letting them get to know each other. I head to the kitchen to make cocktails, eavesdropping the whole while.

"Hi, Carrie," he says, his voice deep and husky. "I've heard all about what a naughty girl you are," and that's the last thing I hear as I fumble with the ice cubes. I pour us all sodas, nixing the alcohol, and quickly hurry back. I almost drop the glasses when I see them kissing, his denim-clad leg thrust between her thighs, pressing upward as she pushes downward. He suckles her lower lip, tugging it between his teeth. I set the glasses down on coasters, and he looks over and gives me a little smile. "You have good eyes, my dear, very good eyes," he says, and pulls back enough so we can both see how swollen his cock is. There's no need for small talk, awkward or otherwise, and things are moving along even faster than I'd anticipated. I follow them up the stairs, watch his hand on her back pushing her up, and I have a feeling he's going to spank her from that slight show of dominance. When she starts to go right instead of left, his other hand lashes out, pulling her close, while the hand that was guiding her back slides easily into her blonde tresses, tugging her head backward to expose her neck. "I'll show you where to go," he says, and she moans in response, giving me a glimpse of hard nipples pressed against the fabric of her dress. I realize she must not be wearing a bra and I feel a gush of moisture fall against my panties.

We reach the bedroom, his hand still tangled in her hair while his other hand immediately goes to his zipper. I step back, giving them a little room to explore but keeping them in my sight. I can see the tendons in her neck straining, her silent swallows as she looks up at him adoringly. She's caught the magic, the fever; that special ability he has to make powerful, sexy women quiver before him, eager to do his bidding. He lets go of her hair so he can push down his pants to reveal his hard, strong cock. He lets the jeans drop to the ground, then sits on the edge of the bed. "Down," he says, pointing, the single word enough to have her instantly on her knees.

This is the moment I've been waiting for, the one I can hardly believe is actually happening. She reaches for his cock with her hand, but he pushes it back and then leans over her, shoving his cock against her cheek as he fixes her wrists behind her back, her hands dangling down just above the end of her spine, right above her ass. "Keep them there. I just want your sweet little mouth," he says, the naughty words making me plunge my fingers into my wet panties for some much-needed relief. I try my best to stay silent, biting my lip as she kisses his cock reverently then licks her way in one long motion from his balls on up to the crown before taking him between her lips. I don't get to see the glory of his cock anymore, but watching her strain to wrap her lips around him more than compensates, maybe because I've been there countless times; maybe because I can hear her heavy breathing in the otherwise silent room, her snorts and gurgles as she swallows him. I peek around and see her rocking slightly, her ass bobbing along with her head, and know she's getting as wet as I always do. I give myself a mental pat on the back for having chosen such a perfect slut as Carrie, as my fingers dive inside my slit. It's hard to tell who'll be offended and who'll be turned on by the chance to bang your boyfriend, you know.

She's got his entire cock shoved down her throat, and her eyes gaze up at him, waiting for his next instruction. She keeps her mouth there, nudging the base, her lower lip flush with his ball sac, until she needs air, and then she slowly rises upward, unveiling his glistening cock for me. I add another finger, and feel my own breath shoot harshly out of my nose, my nostrils surely flared like a horse's, my noises of arousal joining hers.

Carrie starts writhing up and down, faster and faster; and Kyle, who's been trying to maintain a stoic expression, can't help but part his lips, his eyes starting to glaze. She's moaning now, her fingers twitching at their imposed exile from her pussy, when he pulls her up again. "You're a fabulous cocksucker, Carrie. I hope you get lots of practice because clearly you just need cock as often as you can get it," he says, his voice husky, not giving away any sense of just how much he's enjoyed her skills. "I think that made you very wet, didn't it?" he asks. He's not talking to me, and yet it feels like he is. I've orchestrated this little game, but they've run with it. They're not putting on a show for me, I just happen to be their audience, I realize as he sits up on the bed, propping his back against the headboard and lifting her dress off to reveal her smooth, naked backside. He hasn't looked at me once, his eyes fixed on her perfect ass curving across his lap. It doesn't matter though, whether they're trying to show off or not. Watching him do all the things he usually does to me, and seeing her react, has my eyes tearing with arousal, the way they do when I give him a really brilliant blow job. I wouldn't call them tears of joy, exactly; more like tears of overwhelming desire, my body's natural reaction to feeling like I might shatter, exploding in a fiery orgasm right there on the carpet. I dare to step closer and perch on a corner of the bed, so I feel it bounce as he lifts his hand and brings it down with a resounding smack on her ass. Her hands have automatically settled above her head, perfectly subservient, and now I see her bring her arm toward her mouth, so she can muffle her own cries as he does the same thing to her other cheek.

Handprints, large and pink, immediately flower on her pale skin, but he just keeps on going until her ass is totally his, marked by his smacks. I note the way her body moves slightly, her legs widening, her ass arching higher to make the most of his smacks. Soon even her arm can't muffle her sounds. He's had his hand pressed against her lower back, keeping her still so she can fully absorb his smacks, but at her cries, he moves to shove four fat fingers into her mouth. She immediately starts suckling them, as if starved, her face rocking against his invading fingers. This is all way too much for me, and I get up and grab my favorite vibrator. I briefly wish it were one of those small, silent ones, but those have never really done the trick for me. This is a dual-action powerhouse, and I lay it in front of me and hump it, sliding it inside me so I'm pretty much sitting on it before I let it start buzzing. As Carrie sucks and gets spanked, I let the toy whir against my clit and tumble inside my pussy, bringing me to a powerful climax in moments. Carrie turns her head and watches me, her eyes glazed over as he keeps on spanking her. Finally, he pauses, and the lack of noise suffuses the air. I'm spent, and I turn the vibe off. He slides his fingers out of her mouth, but when she whimpers, Kyle offers her his thumb, and she sucks it like a child.

He rubs his hand along her hot skin, then looks up at me, beckoning me forward. I inch closer, so I'm sitting on my knees, which are just grazing her hip. He reaches for my hand, and lets me feel just how warm he's made her ass. I rest my hand there, gently curving my fingers into her sore flesh, while he dips lower, bringing two fingers into her hole. I stare blatantly, so close up, as they emerge covered in her juices, and I hear her sucking on his thumb, gurgling almost as his fingers torment her pussy. He adds a third finger and she cries out. "I think Carrie's ready for my cock, don't you, Sarah?" he asks me, though it's largely rhetorical—if he wants to fuck her right now, he will, and all three of us know it. When he says this, she buckles against him, and he pushes deeper, twisting his fingers around, making her come while I feel her body tremble below me.

Usually he likes to be on top, doggy-style being his favorite, so I assume it's as a favor to me that he lies back against the pillows, sinking down so he's flat on the bed, and turns her around so she's on top of him. He pushes her up so she's straddling him, her hips near his, then nods toward me. I scurry to get a condom, then hand it to her, watching as he holds the base of his cock and she rolls the latex sheath along his bulging length. Her face is serious, full of concentration as she unrolls it. I'm back in the corner of the bed, my body heating up again as she completes her mission and climbs on top of him. I watch from behind, see her reddened ass as it rises up and down along his cock. I let my fingers drift to my cunt, but the urgency isn't there anymore. My fingers lazily part my lips, simply feeling the blood gently swirling below as he keeps his hands on her hips and guides her.

They're not too loud, so all I hear is the slapping as their bodies rub together. I'm suddenly wiped out, exhausted in a way only orgasm can make me, and I lie down next to Kyle, my head on an adjacent pillow, as Carrie smiles at me, her perfect breasts bobbing along with the rest of her. When his hands move around to cup her ass, squeezing it firmly and then pulling her cheeks apart, she pitches forward, tumbling on top of him and smothering my boyfriend with her blonde hair. A few strands land on me, tickling until she lifts her head and shakes them behind her. They kiss; a slow, passionate meeting of the lips as they grind together. I shut my eyes for a moment and find the image of them seared into my mind, captured indelibly. I purr without meaning to, open my eyes to find him sitting up, pushing her onto her back, and sliding out. He takes off the condom, tossing it to the ground as he now climbs on top of her. I don't know what he's doing at first until I see her hold her breasts together, and he slides between them. He spits into his hand to lube up his cock, then puts it back into her titty tunnel, and she pushes them tightly together. "Come on my tits," she says, her gaze fixed on his swollen head riding ever closer to her mouth as he thrusts in and out of her. She doesn't have to do much to get him to spurt, and when he does, I watch his hot lava arc over her body, then land all along her chest, leaving her covered in his white mess. He grunts, then jerks the last few droplets out of his dick before getting up to wash off.

Kyle's never much of a talker right after he's come. I'm still absorbing all of what's happened, my mind adrift as Carrie stares back at me lazily. I'm about to ask what she thought when she says, simply, "You were right. It's perfect," then smears his cream all over her.

I guess if there's any lesson to be learned it's that you shouldn't gloat over your prized possessions, be they a mansion in Malibu, a sleek sports car, or your boyfriend's killer cock. The best things in life, the ones that truly matter, aren't meant to be hoarded, they're meant to be shared. I'll probably lease out Kyle's cock again, maybe for our anniversary, but for now, I'm gonna spend some time savoring his perfect cock all by myself.

ABOUT THE AUTHORS

TARA ALTON's erotica has appeared in *The Mammoth Book of Best New Erotica, Best Lesbian Erotica 2006, Best Women's Erotica, Hot Women's Erotica, Clean Sheets* and *Scarlet Letters*. She lives in the Midwest and writes erotica because that is what is in her head, and it needs to come out. Check out her website at www.taraalton.com.

TENILLE BROWN's writing is featured in such anthologies as *Amazons: Sexy Tales of Strong Women; Glamour Girls: Femme/Femme Erotica* and the projects *Ultimate Undies; Sexiest Soles* and *African American Women Writers: An A to Z Guide*. She keeps a daily blog on her website, www.tenillebrown.com.

M. CHRISTIAN is the author of the critically acclaimed and best-selling collections *Dirty Words, Speaking Parts* and *The Bachelor Machine*. He is the editor of twenty anthologies including

Amazons, Confessions, and *Garden of the Perverse* (all coedited with Sage Vivant), and *Blood Lust* (with Todd Gregory). His short fiction has appeared in over two hundred publications including *Best American Erotica, Best Gay Erotica, Best Lesbian Erotica, Best Transgendered Erotica, Best Fetish Erotica, Best Bondage Erotica* and...well, you get the idea. His first novel, *Running Dry,* is available now from Alyson Books.

ERICA DUMAS' short erotica has appeared in the *Sweet Life* series, the *Naughty Stories from A to Z* series and numerous other anthologies. She lives with her lover in Southern California, where she is currently at work on a short-story collection and an erotic novel. She can be contacted at ericamdumas@yahoo.com.

SHANNA GERMAIN is a freelance writer based in Portland, OR. Her work has appeared in a wide variety of books, magazines, newspapers and websites, including *Aqua Erotica; Best American Erotica 2007; Best Bondage Erotica 2; Luscious; Rode Hard, Put Away Wet* and *Slave to Love.* When not writing erotica, she spends time teaching, traveling and continually searching for that elusive grail, the perfect orgasm. You can read all about her online at www.shannagermain.com.

DEBRA HYDE's erotica leaves no orientation or erotic taste untouched, as evidenced in such recent anthologies as *Aqua Erotica 2; Lips Like Sugar: Erotic Fantasies by Women; Best Lesbian Erotica 2006* and *Out of Control: Hot, Trashy, Man-on-Man Erotica.* Debra keeps the long-running weblog, Pursedlips.com, and its companion podcast, *Pursed Lips, Speaking.*

STAN KENT is a chameleon-hair-colored, former-nightclub-owning rocket scientist and author of erotic novels. Stan has penned nine original, unique and very naughty works including the *Shoe Leather* series. Selections from his books have been featured in the *Best of Erotic Writing* collections from Blue Moon. Stan has hosted an erotic talk show night at Hustler Hollywood for the last five years. The *Los Angeles Times* described his monthly performances as "combination moderator and lion tamer." To see samples of his works and his latest hair colors, visit Stan at www.StanKent.com or email him at stan@stankent.com.

CATHERINE LUNDOFF lives in Minneapolis with her marvelous girlfriend. She is the author of a collection of lesbian erotica, *Night's Kiss*, and various stories which have appeared in such anthologies as *Blood Surrender*, *Simulacrum*, *Kenoma*, *The Mammoth Book of Best New Erotica 4*, *Ultimate Lesbian Erotica 2006*, *Amazons*, *Lust for Life* and *Best Lesbian Erotica 2006*.

SOPHIE MOUETTE is the pseudonym of two professional writers who also publish solo work in erotica, science fiction/fantasy and other genres under other names. Sophie's publications include an erotica novel, *Cat Scratch Fever*, and short fiction in the anthologies *Best Women's Erotica 2005*, *Sex...in the Sports Club*, *Sex...in the Kitchen*, *Sex...in Uniform* and *Sex...on the Move*.

HEATHER PELTIER is a San Francisco Bay Area based writer and educator whose writing has appeared in *Good Vibes* magazine and numerous anthologies. She is currently working on an erotic novel about the hospitality industry.

RADCLYFFE is the author of over twenty lesbian romances, the *Erotic Interlude* series (*Change of Pace, Stolen Moments,* and *Lessons in Love,* edited with Stacia Seaman), and selections in multiple anthologies including *Call of the Dark* and *The Perfect Valentine, Best Lesbian Erotica 2006, After Midnight, First-Timers, Ultimate Undies* and *Naughty Spanking Stories 2.* She is the recipient of the 2003 and 2004 Alice B. Readers' Award, a 2005 Golden Crown Literary Society Award-winner in both the romance category (*Fated Love*) and the mystery/intrigue/action category (*Justice in the Shadows*), and a 2005 Lambda Literary Award finalist in the romance, mystery, and erotica categories. Her latest novels include *Turn Back Time* and *Promising Hearts* (2006). She is also the president of Bold Strokes Books, a lesbian publishing company.

Erotica by **TERESA NOELLE ROBERTS** has appeared in *Sexiest Soles, Secret Slaves, Ultimate Undies, Best Women's Erotica 2004* and *2005,* FishNetMag.com, *Garden of the Perverse* and many other publications. She is also one of the two coauthors behind the pseudonym Sophie Mouette. When not immersed in writing erotica and erotic romance, Teresa is a poet, belly dancer and medieval reenactor.

THOMAS S. ROCHE is the author of more than four hundred short stories that have appeared in magazines, websites, and anthologies including *The Best American Erotica* series and the *Best New Erotica* series. His books include two short-story collections as well as three volumes of the crime-noir series *Noirotica,* four volumes of dark fantasy/horror fiction, *His* and *Hers* (which he cowrote with Alison Tyler) and *Naughty Detective Stories from A to Z.* A photographer and community sex educator as well as a writer, Roche pretends to reside in the San Francisco Bay Area but in fact lives online at *Skid Roche* (www.skidroche.com), at his weblog *Pulp Friction* (http://pulpfriction.typepad.com), and at *Eros Zine* (www.eros-zine.com), where he is managing editor.

Dominic Santi is a former technical editor turned rogue whose stories have appeared in many dozens of anthologies and magazines, including *Best American Erotica 2004; Best Gay Erotica 2000 and 2004; Best of Best Gay Erotica 2; Freshmen: The Best; His Underwear* and many volumes of *Friction*. Santi's latest book is the German collection *Kerle im Lustrausch—Horny Guys*. www.nicksantistories.com.

Simon Sheppard is the author of *In Deep: Erotic Stories*, the award-winning *Hotter Than Hell and Other Stories, Sex Parties 101*, and *Kinkorama: Dispatches From the Front Lines of Perversion*. His work has also appeared in over 175 anthologies, including many editions of *Best American Erotica* and *Best Gay Erotica*, and he writes the column "Sex Talk." His current project is a historically based treasury of queer porn. He lives in San Francisco, and hangs out voyeuristically at www.simonsheppard.com.

Sage Vivant operates Custom Erotica Source, where she writes tailor-made erotic fiction for individual clients. She is the author of *Your Erotic Personality* and the novel *Giving the Bride Away*. With coeditor M. Christian, she has edited *Confessions, The Best of Both Worlds, Amazons, Garden of the Perverse* and *Leather, Lace and Lust*. Her stories have appeared in numerous anthologies.

Saskia Walker (www.saskiawalker.co.uk) is a British author who has had erotic fiction published on both sides of the pond. You can find her work in many anthologies, including most recently *Best Women's Erotica 2006*, *Red Hot Erotica*, *Slave to Love*, *Secrets* volume 15, *The Mammoth Book of Best New Erotica* volume 5, and *Stirring Up a Storm*. Her longer work includes the novels *Along for the Ride* and *Double Dare*.

Kristina Wright is a full-time writer living in Virginia. She holds a BA in English and is pursuing an MA in Humanities. Her erotic fiction has appeared in over thirty anthologies, including four editions of the Lambda Award-winning series *Best Lesbian Erotica* and *The Mammoth Book of Best New Erotica*, volume 5. For more information about Kristina's life, writing and academic pursuits, visit her website, www.kristinawright.com.

ABOUT THE EDITORS

RACHEL KRAMER BUSSEL is a prolific erotica writer, editor and blogger. She serves as senior editor at *Penthouse Variations* and writes the "Lusty Lady" column for *The Village Voice*. Her books include *Naughty Spanking Stories from A to Z 1* and *2*, *First-Timers*, *Up All Night*, *Ultimate Undies*, *Sexiest Soles* and *Glamour-Girls: Femme/Femme Erotica*, among others. The year 2007 sees the release of *He's on Top* and *She's on Top*, companion erotica anthologies dedicated to the thrill of dominance, and *Sex & Candy: Sugar Erotica*. Her writing has been published in over sixty anthologies, including *Best American Erotica 2004* and *2006*, as well as *AVN*, *Bust*, Cleansheets.com, *Diva*, *Girlfriends*, *Playgirl*, Mediabistro.com, *New York Post*, *San Francisco Chronicle*, *Punk Planet*, and *Zink*. She hosts In the Flesh Erotic Reading Series and gets off on watching people eat cupcakes, among many other fun activities. www.rachelkramerbussel.com

Called "a trollop with a laptop" by *East Bay Express*, **ALISON TYLER** is naughty and she knows it. Over the past decade, Ms. Tyler has written more than twenty explicit novels, including *Learning to Love It*, *Strictly Confidential*, *Sweet Thing*, *Sticky Fingers* and *Something About Workmen* (all published by Black Lace), as well as *Rumors*, *Tiffany Twisted*, and *With or Without You* (Cheek). Her novels and short stories have been translated into Japanese, Dutch, German, Italian, Norwegian and Spanish. She is the author of *Exposed*, a collection of erotic fiction (Cleis Press). She is the editor of *Batteries Not Included* (Diva); *Heat Wave*, *Best Bondage Erotica* volumes 1 & 2, *The Merry XXXmas Book of Erotica*, *Luscious*, *Red Hot Erotica*, *The Happy Birthday Book of Erotica*, *Caught Looking* (with Rachel Kramer Bussel), *Slave to Love* and *Three-Way* (all from Cleis Press); *Naughty Fairy Tales from A to Z* (Plume); and the *Naughty Stories from A to Z* series, the *Down & Dirty* series, *Naked Erotica*, and *Juicy Erotica* (all from Pretty Things Press). Please visit www.prettythingspress.com.

Ms. Tyler is an innocent exhibitionist, but a wicked voyeur.